STEVEN B. FRANK

HOUGHTON MIFFLIN HARCOURT

BOSTON   NEW YORK

"Wishes for Alix" by James Emanuel on page 42
reprinted by permission of Broadside Lotus Press.

www.hmhco.com

The text was set in Apollo.

Library of Congress Cataloging-in-Publication Data
Names: Frank, Steven, 1963– author.
Title: Armstrong and Charlie / written by Steven B. Frank.
Description: Boston : Houghton Mifflin Harcourt, [2017] | Summary:
"During the pilot year of a Los Angeles school system integration program,
two sixth grade boys, one black, one white, become best friends as they
learn to cope with everything from first crushes and playground politics
to the loss of loved ones and racial prejudice in the 1970s."
—Provided by publisher.
Identifiers: LCCN 2016014199 | ISBN 9780544826083 (hardcover)
Subjects: | CYAC: Race relations—Fiction. | Best friends—Fiction. |
Friendship—Fiction. | School integration—Fiction. | Schools—Fiction. |
African Americans—Fiction. | Jews—United States--Fiction. | Los Angeles
(Calif.)—Fiction. | BISAC: JUVENILE FICTION / Historical / United States
/ 20th Century. | JUVENILE FICTION / Social Issues / Prejudice & Racism. |
JUVENILE FICTION / People & Places / United States / African American. |
JUVENILE FICTION / Social Issues / Friendship. | JUVENILE FICTION /
Family / General (see also headings under Social Issues).
Classification: LCC PZ7.1.F746 Ar 2017 | DDC [Fic]—dc23
LC record available at https://lccn.loc.gov/2016014199

Manufactured in the United States of America
DOC 10 9 8 7 6 5 4 3 2 1
4500641600

For Mia Frances,
who hadn't arrived in time for the last one;
and for Julie, who got her here.

If someone draws a circle and leaves you out,
you draw a bigger circle and include them in it.

—Maya Angelou's mother, Vivian Baxter, as quoted in
Great Food, All Day Long *by Maya Angelou*

· 1 ·

AN OPPORTUNITY

Charlie

"GUYS, WE SHOULD GO IN. It's a school night."

"Shut up, Charlie."

"Why'd you have to mention *that?*"

"Yeah, Killjoy Charlie. You just ended our summer vacation."

Like it's *my* fault the earth spins? I brace for a tornado of punches. Instead I hear Keith say, "Charlie Ross is right. It's getting dark."

Capture-the-flag ends in a tie and we all head for home. You can hear air conditioners humming from side yards and crickets chirping from trees. Someone kicks an empty Coke bottle into the street. It sounds like a ringing bell.

You can't hear much talk, though. We're all thinking about *you-know-what* starting *you-know-when*. Most summers I look forward to *you-know-what*. But this year I'm starting sixth grade. If I start sixth grade, chances are I'll finish it. And when I do, I'll get older than my older brother.

"See you guys at the bus stop tomorrow," I say.

"Won't see me," says Bobby Crane.

"Won't see me," says Mike Applebaum.

"Or me," says Brett Deitch.

"Why not?" I ask.

"I'm going to Buckley."

"I'm going to Carpenter."

"I'm going to El Rodeo."

Buckley is a private school in Sherman Oaks. Carpenter's a public one in Studio City. El Rodeo is in Beverly Hills.

That's three out of my four friends in the neighborhood changing schools. I turn to Keith, the one I look up to most.

"I'll see *you* at the bus stop, won't I, Keith?"

Keith has sandy blond hair, fair skin with freckles, and sea blue eyes. He carries a pocketknife in his jeans, started wearing puka shells way before they were popular, and lives in the pillow thoughts of practically every girl in Laurel Canyon. He calls us by our first and last names, which can make even a short kid like me feel tall.

"'Fraid not, Charlie Ross. I'm going to Carpenter this year. We gave my aunt's address in Studio City so I don't have to go to Wonderland."

"What's wrong with Wonderland?"

"My mom says it's going downhill."

2

"She say why?"

"Nope. Just that it's a good time to be movin' on. But don't worry, man. I'll still catch you around the neighborhood."

"Cool," I say, as in *No big deal*. But what I feel is cold. Like they all just ditched me.

Armstrong

The trouble with white people is, they're white. It's what I try to tell Mama when she informs me I'll be attending a new school.

"What's wrong with my old one?"

"It's segregated," Daddy says.

"How so? Black kids sit on one side of the schoolyard. Black kids on the other."

"And where do the white kids sit?"

"Only white kid at Holmes is the one in Miss Silverton's belly," says Charmaine, my big sister third from the top.

"That's segregated. And the Supreme Court has said it's time for black and white to blend."

I don't see why. It's not like we're going to rub off on them.

"Where is this new school?"

"In the Hollywood Hills," Mama says.

Hollywood Hills sounds like I'm going to be a movie star. I check myself in the shine of the toaster. Look like a young Sidney Poitier. Start practicing my autograph on the plate.

"How's he going to get there?" Lenai, the oldest, asks. "We don't have a car." She's the practical one. Parent Number Three, we call her, behind her back.

"He won a spot on the bus."

Two slices of toast pop up like eyebrows. Two eyebrows —mine—pop up like the crusts on that toast. How can I win what I didn't even try for? Then Daddy says they tried for me. Signed me up for a new program.

"Opportunity Busing, it's called. You got the last spot."

"I see," I say. "And what time in the morning will my alarm clock have the opportunity to ring?"

"Five thirty. Bus comes at six fifteen."

All five of my big sisters bust up. Lenai, who hardly ever smiles, is laughing. Cecily the Dreamer, always lost in the drawings she does, looks up from her sketchbook, laughing. Charmaine, boy crazy and bull stubborn, is laughing. Nika and Ebony, identical twins born a year before me, who like to fool the world as to who is who, are laughing. All five of them are laughing. Laughing at me.

Last year I got to sleep till seven. They know I need my beauty rest.

"What's the name of this school?" I ask.

"Wonderland."

"*Wonderland?* You're sending me to a school called *Won-derland?*"

"What difference does it make what it's called?" Daddy says in a tone like a loaded gun.

"It's the difference," I say, "between a boy who gets jumped and one who gets left alone. Can you see me stepping off that bus at the end of the day? Kids around here be all, *Yo, Armstrong, we hear you're going to a new school. That's right. What's it called? Wonderland. Wonderland? Say, Alice, what's it like down that hole?*"

"That's exactly why we're sending you. To get away from ignorance like that."

"Well, I'm not going," I say, arms locked across my chest. You got to be firm with people. Especially parents.

Blam! Daddy's fist comes down hard on the table. That's my cue to jump up and run. I've got the advantage when I'm on my feet 'cause he left the one leg in Korea.

"Armstrong, sit down on this chair!"

Daddy picks up the chair, slams it to the floor. *Crack.*

"Ain't no chair now, Daddy. It's a three-legged stool."

"*Isn't a* chair. And that's nothing some wood glue and a clamp can't fix."

I squat on that three-legged stool like I'm in a public toilet afraid to make contact with the seat. Start praying for this to be a short talk.

"Did Rosa Parks give up her seat on the bus?"

"No, sir."

"Then why are you so quick to give up yours?"

There he goes again, bringing up some hero of black history. Every time I sass him, he throws back a legend in my face. How am I supposed to grow up brave like Jackie Robinson, wise like Thurgood Marshall, or strong like Mohammad Ali when they're all looking down at me from Daddy's high shelf?

My legs wobble and burn. I can only catch every third word.

Courage . . . country . . . pride.

In the shine of the toaster, the future movie star starts to sweat.

Change . . . chance . . . pushups.

Pushups?

"No, sir, no pushups for me. I heard everything you said."

"Then you'll go to Wonderland?"

"Yes, sir. I will follow the White Rabbit down the hole."

"Good. Now hop along and do your chores."

I should've run while I had the chance.

Charlie

The leading cause of death for kids between ten and fourteen is unintentional injuries. Freak accidents like getting hit by a car, riding your bike off a cliff, or sticking a fork in a light socket. With statistics like those, why am I sitting in a tree?

Andy called it our Thinking Tree. Its botanical name is acacia, which is what Dad called its twin that blew over once in a storm.

"Boys," he said, firing up his chain saw, "I'm going to need a little help bundling up the acacia." Andy and I had been playing Battleship on his bedroom floor. We looked out the window and saw this massive tree lying in the yard. It had fallen all the way to the front door. "I'll cut up the branches. You bundle and drag them to the curb." Dad tossed Andy a ball of twine. "And remember, boys, do a man's job."

We were boys and men in one breath. Andy put on his ski mask, goggles, parka, and gloves. I wore shorts and a tennis shirt. By nighttime I was squirting Bactine over my arms and legs, Andy was wheezing from an allergy attack, and Mom was combing tiny green bugs from our hair. Tree bugs, we called them. The next morning I found one up my nose.

From the fifth branch of my Thinking Tree, I can see the streetlight by our house. It hasn't come on yet, so I'll sit here and watch until it does. Any time you see the streetlight come on, Andy always said, you're guaranteed good luck the next day.

I wonder why all my friends are changing schools. Do their parents know something mine don't, like we're getting a new principal who'll double the homework and cut the field trips in half? Have all the good teachers gotten better jobs someplace else? Or is there a toxic substance leaking into the water supply, and all the kids who stay at Wonderland will die from accidental poisoning?

Last year in the United States, more than six hundred kids died from accidental poisoning.

Dad's Vespa comes rumbling home from the Mulholland Tennis Club. He's been spending most of his free time up there, playing tennis or gin rummy with his friends. On weekends especially, he'll finish breakfast and say, "Well, I'm going up to the Club." And he vanishes on the Vespa.

The garage door wheezes up. He backs the Vespa into its slot, then steps onto the driveway.

Everything about my dad makes a big sound. He's got Paul Bunyan feet that rattle the walls when he comes downstairs. When he chews a sandwich, you can hear the lettuce crunch. Even his keys sound like heavy chains.

"Hey there, Dad," I call down from my branch.

"Charlie," he says, looking up at the tree.

Some kids have dads who are dictionaries. Mine's all twenty-two volumes of the World Book Encyclopedia in one brain. Whenever there's something I need to know, I look it up in my dad.

"How come nobody's going to Wonderland this year?"

"You're going to Wonderland this year."

"Most of my friends aren't. Keith's mom says it's going downhill."

"Your mother and I don't think it's going downhill. It's taking a different path. Some new kids are coming."

"From where?"

"A housing development in South Central LA. It's ninety-nine percent black."

The opposite of Laurel Canyon, which is ninety-nine percent white. Not boring white. We've still got hippies living in the Canyon. Rock stars too, like Graham Nash, Joni Mitchell, and Carole King, whose daughter was in Andy's class. And we've got movie producers like Reggie Jones, who lives across the street and throws wild parties with naked ladies in his pool.

Can you blame a boy for peeking?

We don't have many black people, though. There were a couple of half-black kids at Wonderland last year, but that family moved out of the Canyon. The only all-black people I know, besides Mrs. Gaines the Yard Supervisor, are Nathaniel and Gwynne, who work for my dad.

"Don't they have their own schools?" I say.

The streetlight is taking a long time to come on.

"The Supreme Court has ruled it isn't fair to keep black and white kids separate. Our city is trying to bring them together by busing some up here."

"Are they busing any to Carpenter?"

"Carpenter seems to have missed the map."

"So that's why so many families are sending their kids to other schools," I say. "They're racist."

"I wouldn't go that far, Charlie. They're doing what they think is right for their children."

I can't help it. Just for a second, my eyes leave the streetlight to look at Dad's face.

"And you and Mom?"

"We're doing what we think is right for ours."

I look back at the streetlight. Just my luck: it's already on.

Armstrong

As the only boy in a house full of girls with a working mama and a one-legged daddy, guess who gets all the nasty chores.

When my daddy's drips land on the bathroom floor, I get the blame—and the sponge. When the toilet clogs with whatever it is females put down there, who do you think is given the honor to plunge? And the one time we had mouse droppings in the bathroom, did they call an exterminator?

No. They called me, Armstrong Le Rois.

You ever empty out a mousetrap? Most people take the longest shovel they can lift, scoop up the dead mouse—trap and all—and chuck it into a brown bag, then throw the bag away.

I wasn't allowed that luxury.

"Mousetrap costs forty-nine cents," my daddy said. "When's the last time you earned forty-nine cents?"

So instead I had to peel back the metal bar and shake the dead mouse into a grocery bag so I could reuse the trap. It was nasty and I didn't want to do it.

"Can't somebody else empty the trap?" I said.

"Who you expect that to be?"

"I've got five sisters."

"They're too squeamish."

"Mama, then?"

"She sees enough death at the hospital."

"Why not you?"

"I saw enough in Korea. You don't want The Flashbacks to come, do you?"

The Flashbacks are my daddy's nightmares that come by day. He can be in the kitchen making dinner or paying the bills when all of a sudden he starts to scream like a thing in the forest, calling out names of men I never met, shouting words I'm not even allowed to whisper.

When I was little and The Flashbacks would come, I thought they were ghosts in the house. I'd hide under the table and grab hold of my daddy's one leg like it was a tree that could save me from a flood. He'd scream and I'd shake. He'd yell and I'd pray—for The Flashbacks not to touch me with their damp, cold hands.

Soon as the nightmares stopped, my daddy would reach down and lift me into his lap.

"It's just The Flashbacks, Armstrong. I never know when they're going to come."

"Can I help you fight 'em?" I'd say.

"You just did."

Another chore I've got is to help my sisters fold the laundry. It's something we all do together because six kids times their clothes is a lot of clothes. Since tomorrow's the first day of school, everybody wants to start with a clean pile.

Here's a pretty little tank top Charmaine wore all summer. I fold it up and put it on her stack.

Daddy plucks it off.

"That's Charmaine's," I say.

"It's yours now."

He puts it on top of my jeans. A pretty little *pink* tank top.

"I'm not wearing that. It's pink."

"What's wrong with pink?"

"Girl's color."

My sisters all bust up again.

"Armstrong, do your sisters take sewing?"

"No."

"Do they take cooking?"

"No."

"What *do* they take?"

"Shop class with the boys."

"And why's that?"

"'Cause you marched into the school and said your girls can do anything a boy can." *Except empty out mousetraps,* I think but don't say.

12

"And my boy can do anything a girl can, right?"

"*Most* anything," I say, hoping he won't ask for the exceptions.

"Including," Daddy goes on, "wear a pink shirt. Now, this one cost three ninety-nine. When's the last time you earned three ninety-nine?"

But Charmaine's not ready to hand down the tank top. She plucks it off my pile and puts it back on hers.

"I like the way it fits," she says.

"So will the eighth grade boys," says Daddy, putting the tank top back on my pile. Then he reaches over to Cecily's, nabs a top two sizes up, and drops it onto Charmaine's.

"That's my lucky shirt!" Cecily says.

Daddy takes another shirt — this time off Lenai's stack — and puts it on Cecily's.

"What am I supposed to have," Lenai says, "one of Mama's? One of yours?"

"You can have a new one. That's how hand-me-downs work. The oldest gets a new shirt."

And the youngest gets a pink one.

Charlie

Mom has spent the last hundred days mostly in bed. She gets up for important things, like the bathroom or morning coffee. Some days she gets up to shower, and some nights she comes down for dinner, which Lily cooks. Once a week, Lily drags her to the market.

Lily is our housekeeper. She came to America in the trunk of a car and had to pay a *coyote,* or smuggler, to get her here. Her room smells like Olvera Street, where she goes on her days off because Olvera Street reminds her of home. Dad's the only one who really talks to Lily—he took Spanish in high school. Sometimes I listen in when she's on the phone with her family in Guatemala or watching TV. But to me, Spanish sounds like Jiffy Pop.

Mom used to tuck me in at night. Now I tuck her in. The bed smells like perfume plus coffee mixed with today's *Los Angeles Times.* A headline peeks up from under the covers: "Ford Pardons Nixon."

"Tomorrow's the first day of school," I say.

Mom's face crinkles up like she forgot.

"Do you have everything you need?"

Good time to ask. Bullock's closed an hour ago.

"Dad took me shopping. I got new jeans. Went up a size."

She smiles her rubber-band smile. It stretches, but it doesn't curl.

There's nothing worse than losing a child. That's what all the people said when they crowded into our house for a whole week last May. They came with pink bakery boxes and cold cuts from Art's Deli. They all had more or less the same thing to say.

We can't imagine what you're going through.

A parent's worst nightmare.

Buzzer words, I call them. If life were a game show, a buzzer would go off every time someone said them.

If there's anything Eleanor and I can do.

Bzzz.

Thank God you still have Charlie.

Bzzz.

You could sue, you know.

Triple *bzzz.*

There's nothing worse than losing a child.

It must be true. She hasn't said Andy's name since he died.

"Good night, Mom."

"Good night, honey."

She hasn't said mine, either.

Armstrong

"You ever been to the Hollywood Hills?"

"I've been to Hollywood Boulevard. Daddy and I took you and the girls once to the Chinese Theatre."

"I remember I stepped in somebody's footprints."

"Jack Benny's. And I put my hands in Clark Gable's handprints. The ladies' were too small for me."

"Whose idea was it to send me to a new school?"

"Your daddy came up with it first. But I agreed."

"Sisters staying put?"

"Not as many spots for junior high and high school."

"You think those white kids want us to come?"

One thing about Mama, she will never tell me a lie.

"Some maybe do. Some probably don't."

"'Cause we're different?"

"Yeah. But you're also the same."

"How are we the same?"

"All starting sixth grade. All turning twelve. Going through the same changes."

I shrug my shoulder to say I'm not so sure. Also to get the covers off so maybe she'll remember to scratch my back!

A cool breeze comes as Mama lifts my shirt. Her nails do lazy eights down my spine.

"You know, you're not the only one getting on that bus. Otis is going. Alma and Dezzy, too."

"Otis?"

"Yep."

"He's always talking about astrology."

"What's wrong with that?"

"It's stupid, Mama. Like your birthday's got something to do with who you are."

"It's just a hobby, is all. Some people believe it."

"Well, I don't. Keep scratching."

She does for a few seconds.

"Come on, now. Otis is all right."

"I guess."

"You will be too, Armstrong."

It's quiet, and I wonder who she's trying to convince.

"I just hope those white kids keep an open mind," I say.

"Why, are you going to teach them something?"

"Somebody's got to."

Mama's hand stops. "You know, Armstrong, it's not just an opportunity to change schools. It's to change ways, too."

"What's that supposed to mean?"

"Six fights in fourth grade. Five in fifth. It doesn't always have to be Armstrong against the world."

That's gonna depend, I think, if it's the world against Armstrong.

· 2 ·

FATHER'S OCCUPATION

Charlie

THEY COME ON A LONG Crown bus with a round back and hissing brakes, the kind of enormous magical vessel we only get to ride when there's a field trip. There are just ten students by the time the bus pulls into the upper yard. Nine black faces pressed to the windows near the driver, and one more sitting in the way way back, alone.

The door flaps open. The up-front kids all come off one at a time.

"Welcome to Wonderland Avenue School," says Mrs. Wilson, our no-nonsense principal. She's tall but looks even taller in a turtleneck, pearls, and hair spray.

The kids all mumble good mornings to her. Then one of the older kids, who has lighter skin than all the rest, turns back and calls down the aisle of the bus.

"Come on, Armstrong."

The boy in the way way back doesn't budge.

"Armstrong, wake up!"

The boy finally stands, stretches, and moves up the aisle. He comes off the bus like a slow-motion Slinky.

"And good morning to you," Mrs. Wilson says.

"Morning, ma'am," he says. But he might as well be talking to his shoes. They're black and white Keds like mine, only not brand new. The flaps of his bell-bottoms scrape the ground. He's not so tall, but he sure looks solid.

Mrs. Wilson stops in front of the easels on the upper yard. To a Wonderland kid on the first day of school, the easels are like holy tablets. They show the class lists for the year. The name of your worst enemy might be on your list. The name of your best friend might not.

The classes are smaller this year—only forty-two kids in sixth grade instead of the usual sixty. Half will get Mr. Mitchell, half Mrs. Valentine. Mrs. Valentine reminds me of my Grandma Sadie, who died when I was eight. She wears the same blue-and-white dotted dress that Sadie's wearing in a picture on our wall. She wears her hair in a bun, too, just like Sadie did. Mrs. Valentine thinks that kids should laugh while they learn. Her classroom is never silent except during reading time or a test. She bakes pumpkin cupcakes on Halloween and gingerbread hearts for the holiday in her last name. And on the Friday before winter break, she gets so many gifts that she needs help walking to her car.

Mr. Mitchell is Medusa with a beard. One look can turn a kid to stone.

If you remember what I said about the streetlight, you'll know which teacher I've got for sixth grade.

Melanie Bates . . . Shelley Berman . . . Susan Campbell . . . Curtis Earl . . . They stare at their names on Mr. Mitchell's list. Otis Greene . . . Alex Levinson . . . Leslie Maduros . . . Yan Park . . . Armstrong Le Rois. And me. We stand in a quiet, straight line in front of Mr. Mitchell, while Mrs. Valentine's class forms a circle around her, telling stories and making her laugh.

"We're in the same class," I hear a quiet voice say to the kid in black and white Keds.

"I'm not sitting beside you, Otis. You'll copy off me like you did last year."

"I didn't copy off you, Armstrong."

"How come you got a B, then?"

Otis sighs. The boy called Armstrong looks at me before my eyes can jump away.

"What are you looking at?"

"Nothing," I say.

"You're looking at something if you're looking at me."

My shoes. That's what I'm looking at now.

Armstrong

I got the nasty man with a beard instead of the friendly old lady. And the white kids keep staring at us like they're from

Sweden and never seen dark skin. That's all right, though. I've got to remind myself why we're here. To educate these people.

First thing we do in class is find our name cards on the tables. Then we fill out forms. *Last Name, First, Middle Initial. Date of Birth. Place of Birth. Race.*

Really?

I'm next to the white boy who was staring at me earlier. Charlie Ross, it says on his name card. Man, the secretary at this school must still be trying to graduate from it. She doesn't even know how to alphabetize. My last name is Le Rois.

What's that start with?

His last name is Ross.

What's that start with?

So how come we're side by side?

"Mr. Mitchell," I say, raising my hand.

"Yes?"

"Are we supposed to be alphabetized in our seats?"

"Yes."

"Then I'm in the wrong chair. His last name, according to the card, is Ross. Mine's Le Rois."

"You're right, young man. You should be sitting next to Mr. Levinson . . . over there."

Mr. Mitchell points to a table with so many school supplies laid out, you can't hardly see the boy who brought 'em. There's a Dixie Cup full of pencils, a stack of Pee Chee folders, a pile of pink erasers, and not much room for me. But here at our table, Charlie Ross is hunched up way over on his side, respecting my space. So I say I'm fine where I am.

"Get back to your forms, then. Raise your hand when you're finished."

I raise my hand.

"Already?"

"Yes, sir."

Mr. Mitchell comes over to inspect my form. Man smells like tobacco from the corner store.

"You forgot box number seven," he says. "If he's out of work, put *unemployed*."

"Didn't forget," I say. "Just don't like to boast."

"Well, you can't leave it blank."

So while I'm writing down my daddy's occupation, I hear Mr. Mitchell say to young Mr. Ross next door, "That's a big word for a sixth-grader. If you're going to use it, you ought to spell it right. There's another *r* after the *p*."

I'm curious what the big word is, so I look over and, sure enough, it's one I don't know.

"Entre . . . pre . . . neur," I sound out. "What's that mean?"

"Businessman."

"What kind?" I'm thinking maybe the real opportunity of riding the bus up here is I can get one of my sisters a summer job.

Charlie Ross sits up tall now, like he's about to announce the coming of the Lord.

"Medical equipment," he says. "My father rents and sells hospital beds, oxygen tanks, wheelchairs, and commodes."

"Commodes?"

"Portable toilets. For patients who can't make it to the bathroom."

Now, here I am at a place called *Wonderland,* sharing a desk with a boy whose daddy rents porta-potties to folks who do their business in the bedroom. And I'm starting to wonder what side of that Supreme Court decision Mister Thurgood Marshall was on.

My upper lip starts to twitch, which it always does when I'm about to bust up. Then I pretend I've got a cough and bury that laugh in my hand.

"Are you okay?" the white boy asks, real sincere. He's probably going to try to rent me some equipment.

"Allergies," I tell him. "Must be all the trees around here."

Then Mr. Mitchell asks Charlie Ross to take the school forms to the office.

Charlie

Okay, so I didn't go *straight* to the office. I ducked into the boys' bathroom for a peek at the forms. Armstrong — whose handwriting is small and easy to read — was born in Los Angeles on May 10, 1963. He has five sisters and no brothers, and they live in a place called the Pueblo del Rio projects. His mom, Gracie, was born in San Diego and works as a nurse at White Memorial Hospital. The nearest relative not living with him is an aunt in Oakland.

But the scariest thing about Armstrong is his dad. Because from box number seven, I just found out that Theodore Le Rois, born in Opelika, Alabama, on June 10, 1931, is a *professional kickboxer!*

At recess there's a mad dash for the handball court. I get there last and line up behind Armstrong. He's got this comb that looks like a pitchfork sticking up from his back pocket. His T-shirt is tight on him, and his hands look heavy on his arms, like the paws on a rottweiler puppy.

Across the yard Leslie Maduros is shooting carroms with Denise Wynn. Leslie was my last crush in fifth grade, and right now, leaning over the wooden board with that long stick in her hand and her brown hair tucked into her overalls, she's officially my first one in sixth. Denise catches me looking and tells Leslie. I blush and look away.

That's when I notice something's wrong. Instead of Armstrong ahead of me in line, it's the boy named Otis, hands plunged deep in his pockets, head hanging so low it might fall off. Ahead of Otis there's Shelley Berman, her arms crossed in frustration. In front of her are about six other kids waiting to play. And in front of *them,* his chest puffed out like he's already full grown, there's Armstrong first in line.

If there's one thing Dad taught Andy and me, it's to be fair in business, friendship, and games. And when you see an injustice, you don't look the other way.

It's just as wrong to ignore an injustice, Charlie, as it is to inflict one.

So I step out of line and walk up to Armstrong.

"Excuse me," I say, "but we don't take cuts here."

He looks at me for a second.

"Here?" he says.

"That's right. At this school we respect each other's place in line."

"As opposed to the ghetto schools where we don't even have lines? It's just a free-for-all?"

"That's not what I said."

"But it's what you're thinking, isn't it? That we got up at five thirty and rode the bus up here so you could teach us how to stand in line? But the thing is, Charlie Ross — that your name?"

I nod.

"We already know how to do that. It's what we learned in kindergarten, even in the ghetto."

"Okay, I wasn't implying —"

"But while we're on the subject, I feel you should know that I didn't take cuts. *He* gave 'em to me."

Armstrong points to the front of the line, where Alex Levinson stands with his shoulders all hunched over.

"Alex," I say, "did you give Armstrong cuts?"

He shrugs. "I'm not so good at handball."

"But you're in next. You won't get better if you don't play."

"Is it wrong to give him cuts? His first day and all."

"It makes everyone else wait longer."

Alex sighs. "I'll go to the back of the line, then," he says. "I learn better by watching."

Armstrong

The rules, according to Charlie Ross, are no slicies on serves; pops are a do-over; Americans and self-inners are out; winner serves; waterfalls and dead killers count. Well, I just served six games in a row, and here comes this bird of a girl. Looks like she won't be going through her physical change any time this decade. She's so little, so brittle, I can't help but give her the advantage.

So I hand her the ball. "What's your name, sweet stuff?"

"Shelley."

"I'm Armstrong. Why don't you serve? I'll go easy on you."

She pushes her glasses up on her nose, bounces the ball

twice for luck, and serves. I give her a nice high-bouncing return that sets her up for a slicey or a slammer. Next thing I know, her twig of an arm starts spinning around like a rock in a sock. Goes right past the ball and — *blam!* — slaps her upside her own head. Glasses halfway down her cheek now. Skinny butt on the ground.

"You okay?" I say.

"I'm not very good at sports."

"You just haven't found the right one yet."

I help her up, walk her back to the line.

Next in . . . Otis.

The thing about Otis is, he's a pasty-skinned brother. I bet he put black *and* white on his school form. He's quiet most of the time, too. Busy with his astrology books. We get along okay. But sometimes when you start something new, you don't want something old hanging on. That's how I feel about Otis, like he's an old coat I'm fixing to outgrow.

"You want to serve, Otis?"

"That's okay, Armstrong. I'll receive."

Receive. Already he's using some extra syllables around here.

I'll just get him out real fast. That's what Otis needs. I start off with a slammer. He's quick to run it down. I do a slicey. He knows how to return that, too. Pretty soon all the white faces in line are swinging back and forth between slicies and slammers, waterfalls and cross-countries, dribbles and dinks. Then Otis catches the ball and says, "You win, Armstrong." It's like he knows he'll never beat me. Knows he'll never lose, either. And he's so polite, he wants to give the other kids a turn.

Here comes Charlie Ross. I can tell he wants to beat me real bad.

"You wanna serve?" I say.

"Winner serves," he says, handing over the ball.

"Oh, yeah. You the Rules Boy."

I bounce the ball a few times to rest my arm. Besides, I got a hunch about this kid, so I say, "You a mama's boy too, Rules Boy?"

Whisper of a voice comes from behind.

"Leave him alone, Armstrong."

There goes Otis, acting like that old coat.

"Say what?"

"Just leave him alone and play."

"I see," I say. "We've got one white boy sticking up for another."

"I ain't white."

"Then how come you got that pasty skin like the rest of them?"

Otis's eyes droop. My fist shoots out. Stops an inch from his jaw.

"That," I say, "is the color black."

Now I'm ready for this Charlie Ross.

Charlie

Armstrong serves and I slam the ball clear to the back of the court. I slam it for Alex, who got swindled out of his place in line. Armstrong's there in a flash and hits it back. I do my best slicey for Shelley, who whomped herself in the face. And for Otis—well, for Otis I send Armstrong halfway across the yard on a slammer. That ought to teach him to insult someone.

No matter what I give, Armstrong gives back. He runs down my slammer and sets me up for the perfect slicey. I angle it sharp to the left, hoping to catch him on his weak side. But Armstrong Le Rois doesn't have a weak side. He gets there just as the bell rings and waterfalls my slicey.

Now, when the bell rings during a schoolyard game, it's an automatic tie. That's the universal rule. So I let the ball bounce and walk away.

"Say, Ross . . ."

I turn around. And the last thing I see is a blue handball flying toward my head.

INCIDENT REPORT

Submitted by: Edwina Gaines, Yard Supervisor at Wonderland Avenue School

Date of Incident: Tuesday, September 10, 1974

Time: 10:30 a.m.

Location: the handball court on the lower yard

After the end-of-recess bell had rung, I noticed a crowd gathered near a boy who was kneeling and clutching his head. I blew my whistle to scatter the children, then made my way down the steps to the injured party. There I saw Charlie Ross with a handball not far from him, rolling on the ground. Evidently—and I don't know if it was accidental or intentional—that ball had just traveled at considerable speed from the hand of Armstrong Le Rois into the head of Charlie Ross. I asked the boy named Armstrong, "Did you throw the ball at Charlie?" "Mrs. Gaines," he said, "I cannot tell a lie. I did throw the ball at him, but in a friendly after-game sort of way." I wondered out loud and to this boy whether or not he understood the strength of his own arm. And he said, "Well, ma'am, it's possible that it sometimes exceeds the situation."

I then gave my full attention to Charlie, and I must say my heart goes out to that boy who lost a brother. Poor child. It's only been since last spring, and Lord, how he looked up to Andy.

I go on simply to add that this is the first time in my memory that we have had an incident to report on the first day of school.

Charlie

"Charlie, what happened to your head?"

"Nothing."

"What do you mean, nothing? One side is twice as big as the other."

"I got hit by a handball, Mom. It's no big deal."

"Are you sure?"

What does she think I am, a mama's boy?

· 3 ·

TRAINING

Armstrong

MY DADDY'S ALWAYS TALKING ABOUT *when's the last time you earned a dollar ninety-nine?* It's not like I haven't tried. Where I live — Pueblo del Rio — we might get the opportunity to jump on a bus, but we don't have much opportunity for a job.

Friday after school, I'm walking home from the bus stop when I notice old Mr. Khalil sitting on his porch behind a dusty yard.

"Mr. Khalil," I say, "looks like you could use some help with your front yard. I can pull those weeds for you."

Mr. Khalil's been around here since the 1940s, when the Pueblo del Rio was built. His house is on Morgan Avenue, outside the projects, but I walk by every day after school. He's probably near ninety years old. Got them soapy brown eyes can already see into the next world. White beard damp with drool. Always an ice pack on his knee.

"Mr. Khalil?"

His raggedy dog starts *rah-rah-ruffin'* at me. That wakes the old man.

"Huh?"

"I say, looks like you could use some help weeding this yard."

Mr. Khalil sits up a little taller in his chair. Squints the nap from his eyes.

"You know how to pull weeds?"

"It's not that complicated."

"There's a right way and a wrong way. Where do you grab them?"

"At the top," I say. "Then I tug."

"That's the wrong way. You have to grab them down low, wrap them around your hand, and twist them out of the ground. You should hear the roots crack. If you don't hear the roots crack, you'll see weeds again after the next rain."

"I'll grab 'em down low, then. How much you pay an hour?"

"I don't pay by the hour."

"You pay by the weed?"

"Not by the weed, either."

"How do you pay?"

"By the job. And I pay in advance."

This looks like my first opportunity to put some honest money in my pocket. "When would you like me to start, sir?"

"How about right now?"

I give him a big smile and walk through the gate. Raggedy dog comes running up, tail wagging but mouth still *rah-rah-ruffin'*. Friendly or fierce, I can't tell.

"That's Patches. Let him sniff your hand."

This is one ugly dog. Probably named for his missing fur. He sniffs my hand, then licks off what's left of the peanut butter from my PB and J sandwich today.

I go on up to the porch, smile at old Mr. Khalil, and put out my hand to get paid.

"Why are you not getting to work?"

"Well, sir, you said you pay in advance."

"I already did pay."

I look down at my hand. Not just clean, but empty.

"What I paid you with is in your head, not your hand."

"How am I supposed to buy candy with what's in my head?"

"By going around to the other residents of this neighborhood and offering your services as a *qualified* weed puller. And be sure to let them know you get paid by the yard, not the hour."

"How will I know how long each yard will take?"

"You have to calculate. This one, for instance, is fifty by twenty-five feet. How many square feet is that?"

"One thousand two hundred fifty."

Mr. Khalil looks at me. Sometimes you look at a person long enough, you can see into their future. That's how he's looking at me now, like he can see into mine.

"Did you do that math in your head?"

Math in your head is easy if you know your *Schoolhouse Rock!* Twenty-five times fifty is the same as twenty times fifty plus five times fifty. That's a thousand plus two fifty.

"Sure I did. Why?"

Mr. Khalil nods. "This'll be your test yard. See how long it takes. Then when you negotiate, you'll be in a better position. Most kids—and you aren't the first to try—come around here and say, 'Mr. Khalil, I can weed your yard for twenty-five cents an hour.' What they're thinking is, they'll take the whole damn day and earn two fifty. Now, suppose you come round and say, 'Mr. Khalil, I can weed your yard for two fifty.' But you get the job done in two hours' time. How much do you get paid an hour?"

"Dollar twenty-five."

"That's five times what the other boys make. Now, what are you going to do with the other six hours in your Saturday?"

"Weed more yards?"

"Three more, to be precise. At the end of the day you will have earned ten dollars."

"What if I can't get it done all in a day?"

"Then you hire some of those other boys. And guess what you pay them?"

"Twenty-five cents an hour?"

"A dollar a yard. That way you're making a dollar fifty for doing nothing. Plus—and I'm not finished paying in advance—you get a reputation around here as an entrepreneur." (That's a word I know!) "Then you add skills to your repertoire." (That's one I don't.) "How to fix a rotted plank of wood. How to set a post and paint a fence. How to cook a warm meal for an old man. And how to read aloud to one whose eyes are growing cloudy with age."

"How am I going to learn all that?"

"I'll teach you. Soon as you finish weeding my yard."

That's how I start *volunteering* for Mr. Khalil. My daddy says going to him is like going to college.

Charlie

Glazed doughnuts. Fire Stix. Razzles. Pixy Stix. Wax bottles. Bazooka gum. Tootsie Pop Drops. Space Food Sticks. Candy necklaces. Licorice strings. SweeTarts and Appleheads. On Mondays and Fridays, at exactly four in the afternoon, the Helms Man drives his big yellow truck, a bakery on wheels, into Laurel Canyon. He sells fresh bread, cookies, doughnuts, and candy. And when his whistle sounds, my hand somehow finds its way into my mom's purse.

The wax bottles are my favorite. Five for a dime. I always bite off the cherry one first, spit the top into the gutter, tilt my head back, and let the cool sweet liquid dribble down my throat. Then I chew the wax all day long. Especially on the left side of my mouth, where my last baby tooth is taking forever to come out.

"Boo!" a voice calls from behind. I turn around and jump back, but it's just Keith. "Two for flinching," he says, and gives me a pair of not-so-soft slugs on the arm.

"C'I borrow a quarter?"

I flick him one. He says he'll pay me back, but I tell him to forget about it. My treat. (It's really my mom's.)

"How are things at Carpenter?" I ask him after he buys some candy.

"Bitchin'," he says. "It's three times as big as Wonderland. And they've got a huge grass field where we play football at recess. But the best part is the girls."

He grins and gives me two more slugs.

"There's this one," he says. "Oh, my God! Charlie Ross, you'd think you'd died and gone to heaven if you sat where I sit in class. Right behind Jodie St. Claire. A total fox. She's got blond hair that smells like the Canyon after it rains. You think I should ask her to go steady?"

"I don't know. I guess—"

"I'll ignore her for a few weeks first. That keeps them interested."

He tears open a bag of Razzles and shakes some into his mouth.

"How's it going with those new kids?" he says in a candy mumble.

"Fine," I say. "Except maybe for this one boy. Armstrong. He's a bit of a bully."

Keith puts up a hand while he works the Razzles. He chews and chews with his finger still up, telling me to wait 'cause he's got something important to say.

He's chewing so long, I see Kathy Foster, Andy's last girlfriend, ride by on her skateboard. Kathy's in seventh grade at Bancroft Junior High, where Andy would have gone. She has straight blond hair and bright blue eyes and wears overalls with a peace-sign patch. We call her the Skateboard Queen of the Canyon. Her feet hardly ever touch the ground.

Once a week Kathy rides by our house. She slows down, glances in the front yard, and rides on. It's like she's looking for something. Or someone. But she never stops to say hello.

Finally the Razzles turn from candy to gum in Keith's mouth. "I got three words to say to you: kick his black ass."

I nod even though that was four.

"Want me to ditch Carpenter one day and come beat the crap out of him?"

"That's okay. I can handle him."

"You sure?"

"He's not *that* tough."

"'Cause if you don't kick his ass in front of the whole school, Charlie Ross, he'll boss you all year long."

I tell him I've got a plan, not to worry.

I wish I had a plan.

Saturday morning I find Dad in the driveway, washing the cars. He's stooped over a back tire on Mom's Buick Riviera. The S.O.S pad looks ready for the trash.

"Need a hand, Dad?"

"Sure, Charlie. You can scrub the rest of the whitewalls." He gives me a fresh pad from the yellow box.

One thing about my dad, he loves whitewalls. Whenever he sees a new car, if it's got whitewalls he says, *That's a good-looking car*. Sometimes he even says, *Get a load of those white-walls, Charlie. There's an owner who takes pride in his car.* My mom, on the other hand, doesn't even know the whitewalls are there. These days she hardly ever takes her car out of the garage, but when she does, the whitewalls come home a little less white. Sometimes a lot less.

"You've got to put some elbow grease into it, Charlie." Dad lets go of the dry, stringy pad in his hand and takes the fresh one from mine. Within seconds his "elbow grease" — more commonly known as "oomph" — has taken all the scuff marks off Mom's tire.

"Now you try the next one," he says, "and do a man's job."

Which is funny because I'm eleven. But I surprise my-self by how much elbow grease I can work up against my mom's right rear whitewall. Soon drops of sweat are dripping from my forehead onto the S.O.S pad.

"Dad," I say, giving my brow a manly wipe, "did you get in many fights when you were a kid?"

"Oh, a few."

"What about?"

"The usual things. Sports, money, and girls."

"Did you ever stand up to a bully?"

"Once, yes. I was in the navy, and a guy on ship called me a kike."

"What's that?"

"The worst possible word you can call someone who's Jewish. It's the equivalent of calling a black person the n-word. Which stands for *never* to be used. Got that?"

"Got it. So what happened?"

"Well, it all started with the Neverfail . . ."

Our family cake. When my dad was in the navy, he got so homesick that he sent a letter to his mom asking for the recipe, which she sent the next week. He quadrupled it, then quadrupled it two more times, to make a Neverfail that would feed seventy-five men at sea. The scent of butter, eggs, sugar, and vanilla woke the commanding officer from a nap. He wanted to know if they'd struck a bakery in the middle of the Pacific.

The bakery was my dad. He didn't have any powdered sugar, so he mixed cocoa powder and butter and granulated sugar, cooked it for three minutes, and cooled it for seven.

Then he poured it on top of the cake, and it made a pretty good fudge frosting.

The commanding officer got the first slice. He told my dad that if they gave promotions for baking, he'd go from radioman to admiral in one bite. "Now share it with the rest of the men," the CO told him.

My dad sliced up that cake fast, like it was for a kid's birthday party. He passed around pieces—sailor to sailor, navy style—to every man on ship.

I'd heard this story before. But there was another part of the story my dad had never told.

"Every man but one," he says now. "When I offered a piece to this one sailor from Alabama, he said, 'No, thanks. I don't care for any cake made by a kike.'

"I asked him to repeat that. And he did. The two k's in the word hit me like fists."

"So what did you do?"

"I was angry, Charlie. It had been a banner day until then. Now I had to ruin it by getting into a fight."

"And?"

"I decked him right then and there."

"One punch?"

"That's all it took. Your old man learned to box in high school."

"But, Dad, isn't it wrong to get into a fight?"

"Most of the time, Charlie. But some things are worth fighting for."

Armstrong

I sure hope we don't get an earthquake, because old Mr. Khalil has so many books they would bury him alive. A whole wall full, and the ones that don't fit inside the shelves are stacked on top, all the way to the ceiling, all the way to the sky if the roof would get out of the way. He's got stacks against the other walls, too. And a ladder to reach them.

A ladder, and he's past ninety years old!

After I tell him about my first two weeks at the new school, including how Charlie Ross forgot to duck, Mr. Khalil raises himself up from his chair and climbs that ladder like a possum heading up a tree. Then he eases back down with a book of poems in his hand. Turns a few pages and hands the book to me.

"Read that one," he says.

"May your playmates be a song,
may your friends just skip along
laughing you into their game
letting you remain the same
in their hearts and on their lips
even when their fingertips
have to let you go your way—
glad they saw Alix today.

"Who's Alix?"

"A young French girl who helped the poet, Mr. James Emanuel, to write again after a long time when his words wouldn't come."

"Why wouldn't they come?"

"He was disheartened, Armstrong, by all the prejudice here in America. It stopped up his pen."

"And the little girl got it to flow again?"

"She made him a drawing and, in return, asked him to make her a poem. That's the one he wrote for her. 'Wishes, for Alix.' But it could be for anybody looking to make new friends."

The poem makes it sound easy.

"What if they don't laugh me into their game?" I say.

"Then laugh them into yours."

"How, Mr. Khalil?"

"By being who you are, Armstrong. Not who they expect you to be."

Charlie

For the rest of September I give Armstrong as much room on the schoolyard as I gave him at our table the first day. On the basketball court, if he says I double dribbled, I hand over the ball. If he says he was sitting *there* first, wherever *there* happens to be, I give up the spot. If he tells me my *white ass* is in his way, my white ass moves out of it. My goal isn't to avoid a fight but to put it off long enough to get in shape.

I start my training at the Mulholland Tennis Club, a ten-minute walk from our house. Built in 1966 when I was three and Andy was four, it looks like a steel and glass spaceship that landed on the hill above Crest View Drive. There are six tennis courts, a swimming pool, and a dining room with floor-to-ceiling windows that look out over the valley and the city below.

Next to the men's locker room is a gym. It has a punching bag and a set of weights that can challenge anyone, from a boy to an Olympian. The sign says NO ONE UNDER 16 ALLOWED IN THE GYM WITHOUT ADULT SUPERVISION. It's a rule clearly stated in bold print. But if I'm going to kick the ass of a kickboxer's son, the Rules Boy is going to have to break some rules.

My routine is the same every day. I switch on my radio and get to work. First the barbells—ten curls of two pounds each. Next the long bar—up to the waist, then to the shoulders, and finally overhead, like I've seen a Hungarian weightlifter do on *ABC's Wide World of Sports*. From there I go to the bench press and try to lift a little more each time. After one week, I'm up to five pounds on the barbells, twenty-five on the long bar, and fifty on the bench press.

One Saturday I'm on my back, bench-pressing to the sound of "ooga chaka, ooga chaka" on 93 KHJ, when I hear somebody bark, "No kids allowed in the gym!"

I look up and see the grouchiest, grinchiest, nastiest member of the Mulholland Tennis Club: Morley Drecker. Or, as he's known to everyone under sixteen, Baldheaded Booby.

My stack of weights clatters down.

"That's without adult supervision, Morley. Last time I checked, I was over twenty-one."

In limps Annette DeWitt, her tennis racket tucked under one arm and a bag of ice in one hand. She wears a supershort tennis skirt, and she's all skin all the way down to the purple puffballs on her ankle socks. Annette is a friend of my mom's and a member of her consciousness-raising group. They get together once a month while the husbands play cards, and they talk about women's issues.

They got the idea from the first *Ms.* magazine, which my mom keeps on the top of the stack even though it's two years old. On the cover there's this modern-day Hindu goddess juggling tons of household tasks. She has eight arms and they're all busy. One is holding a steering wheel, one frying an egg, one answering the phone, one ironing, another typing, one dusting, another holding a mirror, and the last one holding a clock. Plus she's pregnant.

My mom used to be like that. Super Mom. But since Andy died, she's down to two arms. Sometimes none.

Baldheaded Booby goes out of the gym. Annette sits on the seat of the leg press, holding the ice pack to her ankle.

"How's your mom, Charlie?"

"Okay, I guess."

"We've missed her at the CR meetings."

"Maybe she'll come to the next one."

"She has to. It's at your house."

I take the key out of the fifty-pound stack and slide it in at sixty.

"I can never lift more than fifty pounds," Annette says, striking a match. She lights a Virginia Slim, takes a deep puff, and sees me staring at her cigarette. Last year, forty-one thousand and forty-two people died from chronic lung diseases. Cigarette smoking was the leading cause.

She blows out the smoke as far from me as she can.

"I started at twenty, two weeks ago," I say.

"Now you're up to sixty. That's impressive, Charlie."

"Well, I'm in training," I say, hoisting the stack of weights. A small window opens, and I can see the glowing tip of Annette's cigarette. "For a fight."

She blows out a long, thin stream of smoke while I tell her all about the new kids at Wonderland, especially Armstrong and how he's been trying to boss us. Then I set down the weights, sit up, and lean so close to her that I could take a puff of her cigarette.

"He's black," I say.

I say it in a whisper even though we're the only ones in the gym.

Annette nods as though that explains everything.

"I'm going to stand up to him, though."

I take up a boxer's stance in front of the heavy, hanging

bag. My dad has shown me a few moves—a head fake followed by a right hook, a double jab with the left, an elbow for when you're in close.

Annette watches me. Watches and puffs. Then she says, "It can't be easy for him, coming to a new school far from home. Imagine if you'd been bused to his neighborhood."

"My parents would never let that happen." I fling a right jab at the bag.

"No, I don't suppose they would."

She stabs her cigarette into the loopy *M* of the Mulholland Tennis Club ashtray. "Well, my ice has turned to water, Charlie. Remember, that boy is probably as frightened of you as you are of him."

Armstrong, scared of me? Her ankle's not the only thing that's twisted.

· 4 ·

THE BULL AND THE CRAB

Armstrong

LUNCHTIME ON MONDAY, we break into teams for basketball. Ross sets the rules: winners take it out, you call your own fouls, free throws are one plus one. Shoot for teams and do-or-die to start. Game ends when the bell stops ringing.

Teams go like this: Otis, Alma, Shelley, and Ross against Jason Vale, Alex Levinson, Dezzy, and me. That girl Ross is stuck on—Leslie—stands on the sidelines swinging her red click-clacks, which click and clack like a timer for the game.

Because we're roughly the same height, me and Ross end up guarding each other. I score more times than he does, but he passes for more points. We foul each other a lot, but neither one calls it. One thing I notice, he's getting to be pretty strong.

I get the ball and Ross is on me tight. I fake right, spin left. Up for a jump shot.

Swish.

"In yo' eye!" I crow.

Score's 22–20, my team in the lead. Ross is dribbling and I'm guarding him close. We look like a couple of bumper cars at Kiddieland. He bounces off me, spins away, dribbles by. Takes about *five* steps into a lay-up.

Bank-swish.

"Go, Charlie!" the girl with the click-clacks cheers. She's not the only one. Feels like the whole school is rooting for *him*.

"TRAVELIN'!" I yell.

"What?"

Charlie Ross comes marching up all outraged, like he thinks he didn't take those extra steps.

"You were travelin'."

"I'm allowed two steps."

"You took five. And I know you appreciate the rules of the game."

"No way," he says. "Basket counts. Tie game."

"That's not right," I say. "You were traveling, Ross, and you know it. Now, either you admit to the traveling and that basket doesn't count . . . or I kick your ass so bad, you'll be renting equipment from your own daddy."

I don't want to get in a fight with this boy. But if he swings, I'll end it real fast.

Charlie

Armstrong is threatening me in front of my teammates, schoolmates, and Leslie Maduros, whose click-clacks are neither clicking nor clacking. I can't back down in front of her and everyone else. Can't let this newcomer push us around. I think about the gym at the Mulholland Tennis Club, where I've gone from a measly twenty pounds on the bench press to a manly sixty. I hear Keith's voice in my head: *If you don't kick his ass in front of the whole school, Charlie Ross, he'll boss you all year long.*

And my father's: *Some things are worth fighting for.*

I've got the basketball in my hands. All I have to do is fling it in Armstrong's face, and when he puts up his arms I'll . . .

Punch him in the gut!

Kick him in the balls!

Knock him to the ground!

The schoolyard will be ours again.

I look Armstrong straight in the eye, my upper lip snarling, my arms trembling.

He looks at me, calm as *Kung Fu* Caine.

"I might have taken an extra step," I say, just as the bell rings.

Armstrong

"We win!" I shout.

I turn to my team. Raise my hand for high-fives.

But no skin comes.

INCIDENT REPORT

Submitted by: Edwina Gaines, Yard Supervisor at
Wonderland Avenue School

Date of Incident: Thursday, October 10, 1974

Time: 1:05 p.m.

Location: the boys' bathroom

After lunch, when the yard was tidy, I made my
customary rounds of the boys' and girls' bathrooms.
The girls' was quiet and empty. On my way into the
boys', I announced, "This is Mrs. Gaines, stepping
into the boys' bathroom."

I checked to see that the stalls were empty, but
the third one was latched.

"Is someone in here?" I said.

I heard a quick gasp of breath, like a cry suddenly covered up.

"Who's there?" I said. "What's wrong?"

Now, a woman of my height has a hard time
crouching down. But I commenced to leaning over,

and then leaning over some more, so that I might peek under the stall and see if I recognized the shoes. It was a pair of black and white tennis shoes. Keds, I believe. A common brand among the boys.

"All right," I said, "you don't want me to know who you are. That's fine. Except I'm not here to punish. I'm here as a matter of concern of one human being for another. Something must be wrong in a boy's heart if he's holding back tears."

He, whoever he was, made no answer.

"Now, you can come out of there and we can talk. Or I can go round to every classroom in this school and interrupt the teaching to determine which child is out of class."

At this point the latch slid to the left, the door swung in, and I was looking into the face of Armstrong Le Rois.

"Armstrong," I said, "what's the trouble?"

"Nothing, ma'am," he said.

"Then why are you crying?"

"It's a personal matter."

"You're not required to share that with me. I'm just the Yard Supervisor. On the other hand, if there's something I can do to help . . ."

There was a long pause. I waited. I did not want to rush the boy. And it's a good thing too, because when he was ready he said, "Well, Mrs. Gaines, a friend of mine is dead."

"Oh, Armstrong. I'm so very sorry to hear that. Was it sudden? Was it expected?"

"Expected? Maybe by some. But not by me. I saw him just three days before he passed."

"Relative of yours?"

"A neighbor, Mrs. Gaines. He was the oldest man near where I live. I did some work for him."

"How did he die?"

Armstrong's hand came to his chin. "I don't know," he said. "Heart attack, I guess. I'm the one who found him."

"You? What's a boy having to find a dead old man for?"

"It was the day I was supposed to come over and read to him from *Treasure Island*. I knocked on his door and there was no answer. Just the sound of his dog, Patches, barking. So I went around to the rattling old window that he was going to teach me how to fix. I was able to slide it up, and, being small enough, I crawled in. Well, it was an awful thing that I smelled. A worse one that I saw."

"Oh, Armstrong, you'd better stop the story. It's going to upset you too much."

"No, Mrs. Gaines. I need to get it out. And you're

so kind to have this chat with me, I have to make it all the way to the end. I went back to his bedroom. The door was open. I still heard Patches barking. I said, 'Patches, why are you barking at me? You never bark at me anymore.' So I pushed open the door a little wider, and there was Mr. Khalil lying in the bed. And there was Patches standing over him. Three paws on the blankets and one on Mr. Khalil's shoulder. Guarding him the way a dog might stand guard over a toy. Or a treat. That's when I took a closer look at the old man's face."

"And what did you see?"

"Well, it seems that Mr. Khalil forgot to feed Patches the day before he died. And during that day and a half, the dog must've gotten hungry."

"Yes?"

"He had to eat something."

At this point I staggered back and put my hand on the washbasin to keep me on my feet.

"Oh, child!" I said. "You will not have witnessed that! Lord forbid you carry that image to your grave."

"Well," said the boy, "at least now I'm not the only one carrying it, ma'am."

I have, at last count, forty-seven sick days at my disposal. As a result of this incident, I will be taking one of them tomorrow.

Armstrong

Soon as Mrs. Gaines walks out of the bathroom, I hear a terrible sound.

The toilet flushing.

And soon as the flushing's done, I see a terrible sight.

Charlie Ross stepping out of the last stall. He's got this look on his face that says . . . a) I just had diarrhea, or . . . b) I heard everything you told Mrs. Gaines.

"What are you doing in the boys' bathroom?" I say.

"Something from lunch didn't agree with me."

The answer is a.

"Did you hear what I told Mrs. Gaines?"

He nods his head. Looks like the answer is b, too.

Then he apologizes. Says he's *really, really* sorry. Says he didn't mean to listen in. Says he wanted to show some sign he was there, but he was so caught up in the story, he couldn't speak.

He puts out his hand like he wants to touch my shoulder, but I pull back and glance at the sink to give a hint like maybe he should wash.

After he dries his hands, he looks at me real serious. With grandma eyes when you hold out a boo-boo.

"I'm so sorry about your friend," Charlie Ross says.

I feel something stir inside me. Something I can't keep down. I lean over and check the stalls to make sure nobody else is in here. And when I'm sure we're alone, I let out what I've been holding in.

A confetti pop of laughter. The kind that shoots milk out of your nose if you're drinking and along comes a good joke.

"You believed that? Damn, Charlie Ross, you're way too gullible. It's just a story I made up so I could ditch Mr. Mitchell's social studies test. I was messing with Mrs. Gaines. Didn't think I'd be messing with you, too."

I go on laughing and shaking my head. But Charlie Ross has this new look on his face, like he doesn't think it's so funny.

Then he says, "My brother died in May."

That stops the conversation cold. But I've got to wonder, is Ross just saying that to mess back with me?

"For real?"

"For real."

Now I feel, well, not exactly sorry, but surprised. A boy whose brother died. That's serious.

"For *real* real?"

His head goes up and down. Up and down again. Maybe it's true. Still, he better not run to Mrs. Gaines and say I lied.

"You wouldn't run to Mrs. Gaines and say I lied, would you?"

"No," he says.

I give him the same cold, hard look my daddy flashes me when he's mad.

"I won't tell," Ross says.

"Good," I say, "'cause I got her sympathy now. That's like a Golden Ticket around here."

I start to go, but Charlie Ross's voice follows me to the door. "You don't know what it's like to lose someone," he says. "If you did, you wouldn't lie about it."

I walk out of that bathroom feeling like I just walked out of church.

That afternoon, with Charlie Ross's words still preaching around my head, my feet decide to pay a surprise visit to old Mr. Khalil.

"Mr. Khalil!" I call out soon as I see him on his porch.

His head is bowed down to his chin. Hands folded like the newspaper in his lap. I go on in through the gate. Patches won't bark anymore when he sees me, so I bang that gate real hard behind me.

Mr. Khalil is lost in a nap. At least I hope it's a nap. Mama always says to be careful when you tell a lie. Some lies make themselves come true.

"Mr. Khalil! Wake up!"

Not a peep out of this old man.

I walk right up to his face, lean in close to see if he's breathing. Mr. Khalil's got one extra long hair curling out of his nose. When you're real old, you stop trimming in the small places. If he's alive, the breeze from his breath should make that one long hair dance.

It's not dancing. Looks like a comma hanging from his nostril.

I look at his chest. A live person's chest will rise and fall as part of the regular routine of living. Mr. Khalil's chest is all flat. And stays flat for one one-thousand . . .

Two one-thousand . . .

Three one-thousand . . .

Four one-thousand . . .

I killed him. I killed him with my lie.

Six one-thousand . . .

And then, like he just came up from the bottom of a pool, his chest blows up with a big breath.

"You're alive! Oh, Mr. Khalil, thank God you're alive!"

"Armstrong?" he says, opening one soapy eye at a time.

"Hi!"

"Did I sleep all the way to Saturday?"

"No, Mr. Khalil," I say, laughing because I'm so glad I didn't kill him. "It's Thursday afternoon. I was just walking by and, uh, wanted to see how you are."

"And how am I?"

"You're perfect," I say. "But you take a long time between breaths."

Charlie

At lunchtime the next day I find Otis in th[e] *Sydney Omarr's Astrological Guide.*

"Did you know that in a leap year your personality changes, and for one day everybody acts like they were born under the sign of the next month, not their own?"

"I didn't know that."

"I could do your chart someday, Charlie. If you want."

"Sure."

He opens up this little notebook he carries around. "When is your birthday?"

"July the eighteenth."

"You wouldn't happen to know the time of day you were born, would you?"

"I can ask my mom."

"It'll help me to know your rising sign. That's the one that complements your birth sign, which is Cancer."

"Okay. I'll find out."

Otis looks at me like he's reading my face the way he's been reading that book.

"You know your zodiac animal?"

I shake my head no.

"Crab. They move side to side."

"Is that bad?"

Well . . . if you need to get out of the way of something, it's good. But if you need to stand your ground, it's not."

Otis goes back to his book. I hear him say things like "Uh-huh" and "That's interesting" and "You don't say?" I don't want to interrupt him, but I'm curious about something, so when he licks his finger to turn the page, that's my opening to ask, "What sign is Armstrong?"

"Taurus. The bull. He barrels straight ahead. Lotta times without thinking."

"Is that why he's so mean?"

"It's part of it."

"What's the other part?"

"Armstrong is also mean because he's the youngest and not allowed to fight back against his sisters. Armstrong is mean because at our old school he was considered small for his age, so he had to fight his way to the top. One time some kids jumped him. They broke his arm. And Armstrong is mean because of his daddy."

"What does his father do to him?"

Otis looks at me like that's private. I remember that Armstrong's father is a kickboxer. Does he practice on his only son?

"How come he's so mean to you?"

"We go way back. Besides, he knows I'm a Libra. We like to keep the peace. And we're real quick to forgive."

By now Otis's finger is dry, and I can see he really wants

to turn that page, but before he licks his finger again I say, "One more thing, Otis."

"Yes, Charlie?"

"Is there anyone at this school who can beat up Armstrong?"

"Student or a teacher?"

"Student."

"None that I know of. It might be possible for our teacher, Mr. Mitchell, but I wouldn't bet on it."

Armstrong

Friday afternoons at my old school, Miss Silverton used to read to us. Books from inside her desk. Books from her purse. Books from her coat. She was a library with feet.

I liked the one about the boy who wins the chocolate factory. And the Hardy Boys. A little too white for my taste, but they sure can solve a crime.

Here at Wonderland they've got the wrong idea about reading. Instead of reading from a book, Mr. Mitchell thinks we should read from a box.

He calls it the SRA box. Inside you find shiny plastic cards with a colored band at the top. Green, blue, yellow, orange, red, silver, and gold. Each one's got a different article or paragraph they want you to read. Comprehension questions waiting on the back of the card. We do the questions, then check ourselves against the key from the back of the box. If we get all the questions right on three cards in a row, we go up a color.

Here's something I read on a green card: *A grasshopper can camouflage itself on a leaf. Both are the same shade of green. The insect blends in.* On the back the questions go like this:

A grasshopper can blend in on a leaf because . . .

> *a) the sunlight is in its face.*
> *b) it has the same color as the leaf.*
> *c) it hides under a rock.*

This is the most insulting type of reading you ever saw. The colors change, but the writing stays the same. Words get a little longer, is all. You never see the author's name on a card. I wouldn't put my name on them either.

Meantime, Mr. Mitchell is studying his *Los Angeles Times*. Miss Silverton never did her own business at the desk.

I go up to that box of cards and flip past the yellows and oranges. Pick up a red card. Maybe this is where the stories are.

Mr. Mitchell looks up from the sports section, where he's checking the odds for Sunday's Rams game.

"What are you doing, Armstrong?"

"Looking for something good to read."

"What color are you?"

"Excuse me?"

"What color reader are you? I see your hands up there at red."

"My hand is searching for a story, sir."

"Yes, but you have to make progress to read in the advanced section."

"Well, I have made progress," I say. "I read at the same level as, uh, Charlie Ross, for instance."

"Is that right?"

Mr. Mitchell folds up his *Los Angeles Times* like it's ready for redelivery. He slides back from his desk and strolls over. "Mr. Ross," he says, "Mr. Le Rois here thinks he can read at your level. What color are you up to?"

"I don't know," Ross says. "Red, maybe."

"Red is just two colors shy of gold." Then Mr. Mitchell turns to me. "And you think you're a red reader, is that right?"

"I am if he is."

"Well, if you are, you've been keeping it a secret."

"I was brought up not to boast, sir."

"Were you brought up not to bet?"

"Betting's okay."

"So you'd be willing to bet that you can read at the same color as Charlie Ross."

"Yes, sir. But I'd like to know what it is we're betting."

"Your grade, of course. If you read a red card and get as many questions right as Charlie gets on his red card, I'll give you an A-plus in reading."

"And if he can't?" Charlie Ross asks.

"Then he brings home an F to his mother, who I'm sure taught him not to lie, either."

Terrific. Now I'm in a reading contest.

Charlie

When Mr. Mitchell asks for a volunteer to keep time, the only hands that aren't practically holding up the ceiling belong to Otis, Alex, and Shelley.

"Okay, Jason," he says. Jason Vale, a heavyset kid whose hair grows wild down his shoulders like the ivy on our back slope, gets up from his seat. Mr. Mitchell hands Jason a small stopwatch.

"Ten minutes," Mr. Mitchell says.

"Ready . . . set . . . go!"

I look down at my SRA card. It's a page from *The Boy Scout Handbook* on how to construct a raft. At least that's practical information. I wonder what Armstrong got. I glance at his card: "Parliamentary System of Government in England."

How's that for a fun read? What are we even doing here? It's like Mr. Mitchell is going out of his way to embarrass

Armstrong. For what? Claiming a level, a "color," above his own?

When constructing a raft in nature, the first step is to . . .

> *a) seek level ground.*
> *b) gather wood.*
> *c) unspool rope.*

The manual said the first step is to seek level ground. I choose c) unspool rope.

When gathering wood, you should look for logs . . .

> *a) of equal thickness.*
> *b) of equal length.*
> *c) of the same kind of tree.*

I glance back at the part about wood gathering. It says the most important factor in selecting wood is length. I choose c) of the same kind of tree.

I can see that Armstrong's on the last question when Jason shouts, "STOP! Time's up!"

Mr. Mitchell asks us what card numbers we have. We tell him, and he gets the answer keys from the back of the box. He hands me Armstrong's card and he hands Armstrong mine, telling us to grade each other.

There's this underwater silence in the room as I go over Armstrong's answers. Each time he gets one right I feel relieved, like it's my own test I'm grading. Each time he gets one wrong, it's hard to breathe.

"Well?" Mr. Mitchell says when we both look up.

"He got three wrong," I say. Mr. Mitchell looks over Armstrong's answer sheet. Then he looks at Armstrong. "And how did Mr. Ross do?"

The room goes quiet again. And then Armstrong announces the verdict. "Two out of ten."

"Two wrong out of ten," Mr. Mitchell says. "He beat you by one."

"Two *right* out of ten. Eight wrong."

Otis smiles. Mr. Mitchell plucks the card from Armstrong's hand, thinking there's got to be some mistake. He compares my answers to the key, then hands the card back to me.

"It would appear that Mr. Ross needs to work on his reading," Mr. Mitchell says.

Armstrong

In the boys' bathroom, I don't even wait for Ross to zip up before I shove him against the wall.

"Don't you *ever* cut yourself down for me again," I say.

"What're you talking about?"

"You put the wrong answers on purpose, didn't you?"

Ross tries to look away from me, but I get right up in his

face. "Thought you'd do me a favor. Make the *bus* boy look a little less dumb."

"The contest was dumb, Armstrong. Not you."

"Bad enough I got that man for a teacher. I don't need any charity from you."

"It wasn't charity. I wasn't paying attention."

"Look, Ross, next time we get in a contest, pay attention. Try to win."

"Fine," he says. "I will."

"Try as hard as you can."

"Fine," he says again. "I will."

"Try like your life depends on it."

"FINE!" he shouts. "I WILL!"

"And before you walk out of here, I think you should know that your fly is open."

On my way out, I hear him zipping up.

· 5 ·

FLASHES OF SILVER

Armstrong

LAST YEAR DURING LUNCHTIME, I always knew where to sit. If I sat at Caldwell's table, I would have my ass kicked. But I could have a space over by Jerome and eat in peace. Around here, my ass is not likely to get kicked, but at the same time, I'm not sure where it should land. There's room at Alex Levinson's table, but Otis's lunch box is already there.

There's Alma and Dezzy over by that tree, but why take the opportunity to come to a white school if you're going to sit at the black table? Might as well sleep in. I could eat with the fifth-graders, but I think they're scared of me.

I might try to sit beside Charlie Ross, but ever since he told me about his dead brother, I don't feel right around him. Plus, he didn't respect me in the reading contest.

So most days I eat alone.

About halfway through lunch, flashes of silver start

coming out of everybody else's bag. Charlie Ross is always pulling out the silver. And the minute he unwraps it, I smell chocolate. Ding Dongs most days, but lately he's got these smaller treats he calls Ho Hos. Sounds like Santa's food.

A Ho Ho starts with flat chocolate cake. Then comes a layer of smooth white frosting. The two are rolled up together in a black 'n' white wheel. And if that's not tempting enough, the whole scrumdiddlyumptious thing is dipped in more chocolate! Man, what I wouldn't do to try one!

At the market the other day I told my daddy, "Hey, Daddy, I'd like to try Ho Hos in my lunch."

"Ho Hos cost seventy-five cents a box. When's the last time you earned seventy-five cents?"

Maybe I'll make friends with Charlie Ross and we'll do a trade. I can guess how that's going to go.

Say, Ross, you got Ho Hos in your lunch. Trade you for some celery?

Or *Hey, Ross, you want me to help you with your math homework? Two Ho Hos for twenty problems.*

Or *You know, Ross, I was talking to Leslie Maduros about you.*

You were?

She says she likes you a lot.

She does?

Only trouble is, she's worried you're getting a little chunky.

Well, I have been lifting weights.

Been lifting Ho Hos, too. Tell you what. I think you could get some action with that girl. I will put you on a diet first. Let me hold your Ho Hos, and soon you'll be holding her hand.

Okey-dokey. Here you go.

He'll see right through that scheme.

I could just flat-out ask him.

Say, Ross, what are you having for your dessert today?

A Ho Ho.

Never had one of those. Looks pretty good.

Mmmm hmmm, he'll say. *Sure is.* Then he'll lick the last bit of chocolate off that foil.

It says in the Bible "Thou shalt not steal." But the Bible is the word of God, right? Whoever wrote it down was stealing from the Lord. Making good money off Him too. That's the best-selling book of all time. Don't you think it's worse to be stealing from the Almighty than from chunky Charlie Ross?

On the other hand, if I take what's not mine, Mr. Khalil will kill me with silence. And my daddy will kill me with words.

On the other *other* hand, I really want to try a Ho Ho.

Charlie

The first time there's no Ho Ho in my lunch, I don't give it much thought. Lily probably forgot, is all. The second and third times I'm a little annoyed. I figure we ran out.

The fourth time I curse her. I've eaten half my tuna sandwich, my barbecue chips, the celery and carrot sticks. I've taken the required three bites of my apple. I'm ready for dessert.

But when I reach into the brown paper bag with my name on it, I feel no silver foil. No palm-sized cylinder of joy. What I feel instead is the bottom of the bag, as empty and low as my heart.

That night after dinner, I stand in the kitchen watching Lily make my lunch, like she's a factory worker and I'm her boss. When she drops a Ho Ho in my bag, I peer a little closer into the sack. She looks at me and says, "*Que pasa,* Charlie?"

"You forgot my Ho Ho yesterday."

"*No.*"

"*Sí.* And the day before."

"*No.*"

"*Sí.* You forgot all week."

She looks at me like she thinks I'm making this up.

"*Había una caja entera el domingo. Deberían quedar cinco.*"

Lily tips over the box, and sure enough, five Ho Hos tumble out. She thinks for a second.

"*Tal vez alguen esta robando.*"

"*Robando?*"

She grabs a Ho Ho and sneaks it under her arm.

"Who would steal a Ho Ho?"

"*Quien sabe?*"

That's Spanish for "Who knows?" Well . . . there's one way to find out.

My plan wouldn't be possible without Lily. She has weekends off, and when she comes back from Olvera Street on Sunday night, it's usually with a bag of foods she doesn't even try to translate for the shopping list. Dried chili peppers, powdered spices, and sauces with dancing flames on their labels. She keeps them in her room on top of her TV so there's no chance our gringo tongues'll get burned.

And my plan wouldn't be possible without Andy. When the allergy doctor wanted to put him on weekly shots and charge five dollars a poke in the office, my dad thought that was an "excessive" fee. He ordered a year's supply of syringes from a pharmaceutical catalog, and Mom gave Andy the shots at home. I used to watch as she'd take a syringe, poke its needle into the jar with the medicine, and pull back the plunger, filling the syringe halfway with a clear liquid. Then I'd watch Mom give Andy the shot.

The bad thing about ordering a year's supply of something is, if the person you ordered it for dies, you're stuck with a lot of leftovers.

The good thing is, leftover syringes can come in handy.

Friday morning I'm up and out of bed before my clock radio goes off. I've got this nervous, giddy feeling, like revenge is just a few bites away. In class five minutes before the bell, I take the brown bag with my name on it and set it on the shelf inside our coat closet. As I turn away, I can feel

Armstrong's Ho Ho–hungry eyes on me, but I don't return the look. I wouldn't want to make him suspicious.

To look at it — to touch it, even — you won't notice anything different about the Ho Ho in my bag. It's the familiar foil-wrapped chocolate cake and white frosting rolled up into one treat. You might even unwrap it and sniff around. You'll smell chocolate and sweet cream and nothing more.

But take a bite, and your mouth is in for a surprise.

INCIDENT REPORT

Submitted by: Edwina Gaines, Yard Supervisor at Wonderland Avenue School

Date of Incident: Friday, November 1, 1974

Time: 12:25 p.m.

Location: the upper yard

I was on yard duty at lunchtime today, and the children seemed to be eating their lunch just fine with no incidents to report. But all of a sudden I heard a cry rise up from the crowd, and it sounded like "HOT, HOT! THPITHEY! HELP! WATUH!" I looked over and saw that a crowd of people had formed around a boy whose mouth evidently had made contact with some spicy food. Now, I know there's a packet of hot sauce served with the burritos in the lunch program, but I have had that sauce and there's nothing to it. So clearly this was something that had arrived in a bag or box of one of the students. I could not see who that boy was on account of the crowd, but I could hear his desperate cry. And pretty soon I saw what I can only describe as a fire brigade of students in a line between the boy whose mouth seemed afire and the water fountain, where all three spigots were filling Dixie Cups that were then being passed up the line to the boy. I debated whether or not to blow my whistle and decided to leave it hanging because I did not want to interrupt the relief that was under way. I did, however, make my way along that brigade to the front, where I discovered a boy with one hand flapping like a wing in front of his mouth and the other gratefully receiving cups of water from the line.

That boy was Alex Levinson.

I asked him what happened. His speech was hindered by the swelling of his tongue.

"Thpithey. Thometing thpithey," he said.

"What did you eat today, Alex?"

He answered in two brief grunts of equal duration. I did not understand the words. Then he held up a foil wrapper that anyone here will recognize as the mark of a Hostess product, either Ding Dong or Ho Ho. Judging by the size and shape of the wrapper, I determined it was a Ho Ho.

"Was there something wrong with the Ho Ho in your lunch?" I asked.

"Thometing wong, yeth," he said, "but not my lunth."

"Well, then, how did you get this Ho Ho?"

"I . . . I tayded for it."

"Traded whom?"

"Armthong."

"Armstrong," I said, "did you give this boy a Ho Ho?"

"Yes, Mrs. Gaines, I did. But I don't know how come it lit his tongue on fire."

"Well, where did you get it from?"

And he said, "I cannot tell a lie, Mrs. Gaines. I stole that Ho Ho from somebody else's lunch. But before I unwrapped it, I looked across the table and saw Alex there about to eat some Space Food Sticks. I never tried those. Always wondered about them, too. Seen the ads on TV with the astronauts in space. And so I asked Alex if he'd like to trade. One Ho Ho for all the Space Food Sticks. He said he was tired of Space Food Sticks and would be happy to trade."

"Well," I said, "whose lunch did you take the Ho Ho from?"

And then Armstrong put up his finger like he

was testing the direction of the wind. And down came that finger pointing directly at Charlie Ross.

Whereupon I escorted one boy to the nurse's office and two to the principal.

Charlie

The principal's office is the scariest place on the planet. Before you go in, there's the smell of tardy slips and typewriter ink and the secretary's hair spray. Not to mention the rubbing alcohol from the nurse's office next door. Makes you run a fever even if you're not sick. Meanwhile, you have to wait in those tiny plastic chairs against the wall. The whole world knows why you're there. Then the secretary says in a really loud voice, "The principal will see you now."

You feel like Dorothy walking up to Oz for the first time. Then you step through The Door of Doom.

That's where Armstrong and I are now, on the other side of that door.

"Sit down, boys," Mrs. Wilson says.

We sit in the hard wooden chairs in front of her desk.

Mrs. Wilson looks up from the Incident Report. She lowers her reading glasses and lets them dangle by a chain around her neck. The chain looks strong enough to hang a kid.

"Charlie Ross, do you know what a vigilante is?"

I shake my head because I don't.

"It's someone who takes justice into his own hands," Armstrong says. "Someone who tries to catch a thief by setting a trap."

Armstrong grins at me. Not because he knows the word, but because he knows which one of us it fits.

"That's right, Armstrong," Mrs. Wilson says. Her head turns back toward me. "This isn't the Old West, Charlie. If you think someone's stealing from you, you tell a teacher. You tell Mrs. Gaines. You tell me. Understand?"

I nod. It's Armstrong's turn. It better be Armstrong's turn.

"Armstrong Le Rois, is it ever okay to steal?"

"No, ma'am."

Now I get to grin at *him*.

"Unless . . ."

"Unless?"

"Suppose your uncle is talking about shooting himself on account of he lost his job and his wife ran off with another man. You go and steal his gun and hide it someplace he'll never find. That's stealing in order to save a life."

Mrs. Wilson has a rubber-band smile too, just like Mom. She sighs and says, "An exception."

"Or you steal the getaway car from a bank robber. That makes you a hero."

"Another exception."

"Or your mama's been smoking and you don't want to be an orphan, so you steal her cigarettes and flush 'em down the toilet — to save her life."

Andy and I used to flush Mom's cigarettes all the time.

"Cigarettes are a far cry from Ho Hos, Armstrong Le Rois, and you know it. I *know* you know it."

Mrs. Wilson brings her glasses to her mouth and thinks. The school clock on the wall does its backwards *tick* and then its forward *tock*.

"Armstrong, the punishment for stealing is suspension for a day. Along with a letter of apology to Charlie on why what you did was wrong. Charlie, the punishment for being a vigilante is also suspension for a day. Along with a letter to Alex on why what you did was wrong."

"Just Alex?" Armstrong says.

"Just Alex. You're both not welcome back in school until you show me those letters. Signed by your parents."

I take back what I said earlier. There's one thing scarier than the principal's office: my dad's face when he finds out what I did. He tells me he's *appalled* at my behavior. He can't believe his son could be so *negligent, thoughtless, irresponsible,* and just plain *dumb.*

Each word is a slap in the face. But what he says next is the knockout blow. "What if Alex had been like Andy, a highly allergic child? Do you realize you could have killed him?"

I never thought of that. My father's right. I'm all those things he said I was.

"I wasn't trying to hurt Alex," I say. "I was trying to hurt Armstrong."

"It's just as wrong."

Dad takes a pen and adds "Ho Hos, 4 boxes," to the shopping list. He then announces that Mrs. Wilson's punishment didn't go far enough. A more valuable lesson will be learned if I bring to school, as a "dual token of remorse and compassion," four boxes of Ho Hos—two for Alex and two for Armstrong—which I have to pay for with a day of hard labor at Ross Rents.

"Four for Alex," I say. "None for Armstrong. He's the one who stole."

"And it wouldn't kill you to wonder why."

Armstrong

"It's Monday, Armstrong. Why are you not in school?"

Up on my shoulder sits a fifty-pound sack of Quikcrete, which my daddy made me carry half a mile from the hardware store. He said I'd be spending all of Suspension Day helping Mr. Khalil repair his front porch. "Hard physical labor," he said. "That's what you'll do because you stole."

Hard physical labor is easy compared to what I've got to do now—tell old Mr. Khalil why I'm here.

I try to come up with a holiday he might believe. But Halloween passed and it's a week before Veterans Day. I don't know when else you get a random Monday off, unless you're Jewish like Charlie Ross.

No, the calendar will not get me out of this. I'll give it to Mr. Khalil quick, the way I run in and out of the shower after my sisters use up all the hot water.

"I got s—"

"What?"

"I got sss—"

"Strep throat?"

"Worse than that."

"Staph infection?"

"Worse than that."

"Salmonella?"

"I don't even know what that is. But what I got is worse."

"What, then?"

"Suspended."

"Suspended?!"

"It's contagious. Charlie Ross got it too."

"Why in the world did you get suspended?"

"It's Ho Hos, Mr. Khalil. I've got a weakness for them."

"So you went and stole one."

"No, sir."

"No?"

"I stole five. But the last one I traded for Space Food

Sticks. That's the Ho Ho Charlie Ross hid the hot sauce in. And *that's* how we both caught the same disease."

"Armstrong," Mr. Khalil says, looking at me. "Armstrong," he says again. "You took the easy way. The lazy way."

"Are you disappointed in me?"

"Are you disappointed in yourself?"

Eyes have never been so heavy in a boy's head.

Charlie

Ross Rents is on South La Cienega Boulevard, two blocks north of the Santa Monica Freeway, "so the deliverymen don't lose time on their routes," Dad always says. The neighborhood is mostly black, and whenever he puts a help-wanted ad in the paper, the people who live nearby line up to answer it. That's how Nathaniel and Gwynne came into our lives. Gwynne is my dad's Administrative Assistant, and Nathaniel is the Shop Manager and Transportation Director. Nathaniel is so tall that he has to bend down going through doors.

Most adults greet a boy by messing up his hair or patting his shoulder and saying, "Well, hello there, young man." Nathaniel greets me by name and with something that makes the height difference between us seem small: a handshake. It's no ordinary straight-on shake but a kind of secret shake in three steps. First the hands meet at an angle, like they're about to arm-wrestle. Then they slide into a regular grasp. Then they pull back until the curled fingers of one hand hook onto the curled fingers of the other, like a hinge. One time Nathaniel told me that this is the handshake of black men who think of themselves not just as friends, but brothers.

My job today, Suspension Day, is to polish the wheelchairs, walkers, and commodes that have been returned. Nathaniel's job is to inspect them for damage and do the necessary repairs. There's a bench radio in the store, tuned to 1580 KDAY. Nathaniel's station. No sappy love songs, just ones with a good beat. The music helps me shine six wheelchairs and four walkers by the time noon comes around and Nathaniel says, "Let's break for lunch, Charlie."

At the long bench in the back of the store, we open our brown bags and eat. After we finish our sandwiches, I dig a little deeper in my bag and find a Ho Ho. Unwrapping it, I see Nathaniel glance at it like maybe he wants some, so I break it in half.

"Here," I say. "Split it with me."

"Thank you, Charlie."

Half a Ho Ho in Nathaniel's hand looks no bigger than a crumb. He lifts it to his mouth, then lifts it to his nose. He looks at me and winks.

"My dad told you what I did."

Nathaniel nods and tosses the rest of the Ho Ho into his

mouth. He chews slowly, and I can tell he's got something on his mind.

"Your father's a wise man, Charlie. But I'm not sure I agree with him on this one."

"You wouldn't make me work today?"

"Oh, I'd make you work. But not to reward a boy for stealing."

"That's what I think! If anything, Armstrong should work to buy *me* a box of Ho Hos."

"Or his own."

Nathaniel unscrews the cap on his thermos and pours. The back of the store smells like morning in our kitchen. "Armstrong came on the Opportunity Busing program, didn't he?"

"You heard about it?"

"I read about it in the paper."

"Do you think it's a good idea?"

Nathaniel sips his coffee. He looks at me. Then he says, "I'm against it, Charlie."

"Why?"

"Seems to me, the money they spend to put gas in those buses would be better spent to improve the schools. In all the neighborhoods."

"Don't you think black and white students should mix?"

"Maybe if the buses ran both ways. But I don't see any white students getting up before dawn."

I try to imagine what that would be like. Not just waking up early, but riding a bus all the way out of Laurel Canyon, down La Cienega, past Ross Rents and onto the Santa Monica Freeway toward downtown. After that the bus would head south on another freeway. How far would it go, I wonder.

"I guess it is a long ride for Armstrong to Wonderland every day," I say.

"An even longer ride home," Nathaniel says.

"Because of the traffic?"

"No, Charlie. Because of the way home looks after you've been gone."

Armstrong

Tuesday after Suspension Day, I'm at my lunch table with a peanut butter sandwich.

"How come no jelly?" I asked this morning when my daddy snatched away the jar.

"Jelly is sweet," he said. "Them Ho Hos you took gave your mouth enough sweet to last a lifetime."

So now, just when I'm wishing for some dessert, guess what drops from the sky.

Two boxes of Ho Hos!

"Those are for you," Charlie Ross says.

"What for?"

"It's my punishment for getting suspended. My father made me earn them."

Peanut butter and Ho Hos would be a fine mix. Like a Reese's peanut butter cup, only soft all the way through. And my daddy would never even know.

But peanut butter and Ho Hos *and charity* from Charlie Ross would leave a bitter taste in my mouth all the way to the grave.

"No thanks," I say, and walk away.

· 6 ·

ARM-WRESTLING ARMSTRONG

Charlie

ON THE FIRST MONDAY IN December, Armstrong announces he'll be holding an arm-wrestling contest at the end of the week. The rules, *his rules,* are that he'll sit on one side of a lunch table and all sixth-graders *who think they're somethin'* can line up for a chance to beat him. The entry fee will be twenty-five cents, which you have to drop into a Coke can that Armstrong'll put on the table. If one of us—*any* one of us—can beat him, the entire contents of the can will be ours.

All week long the sixth-graders go without milk. I feel sorry for the milk monitor, who has to carry the heavy tray from the refrigerator to the lunch tables. Most weeks he sells out, and the walk back is a lot lighter. But this week nobody's forking over the five cents a day for a carton of milk. By Friday, when the refrigerator should be empty, it's full. And when our pockets should be empty, they're also full—with five nickels.

Twenty-five cents. The price of glory.

Friday at lunch, Armstrong sets down an empty Coke can: open for business. The sixth-graders—all the girls and all the boys except Otis—form a line. I make sure I'm the last one in it.

By the time I belly-up to his table, Armstrong has brought down forty arms (forty-one if you count the *two* hands he let Shelley use). I feed my nickels into his can one at a time. There's room only for three. The other two rest on top.

"Right hand or left?" he says.

"Right."

Before we start, I want him to know that *this* challenger isn't just another scrawny white boy from Laurel Canyon, but a husky, bench-pressing, whitewall-scrubbing, bad-ass white boy from Laurel Canyon. So I pull my short sleeve up over my shoulder and twist it under my arm like a tank top.

Armstrong looks at my bicep.

"Been lifting wheelchairs, haven't you, Ross?"

"Yup."

"Quikcrete weighs more."

He pulls up *his* sleeve and shows me a bicep three times as big.

Our elbows hit the table and our hands come together. If you've ever had your blood pressure taken, you know how they strap that cuff around your arm and at first it's snug but not too tight, but then the nurse squeezes the little bulb and the cuff gets tighter and tighter until it's a cobra wrapped around your arm. Well, Armstrong's grip is like that. It starts out all friendly and soft, but pretty soon I feel him squeeze my hand like he wants to crush it. But guess what. Tennis has given me a strong grip too. So I squeeze back just as hard. Armstrong's eyes flash at me like he wasn't expecting this. And my eyes flash back because neither was I.

Armstrong

Ross waited till the last minute 'cause he thinks I'll be tired. What he doesn't know is that when you've been twisting weeds by the bottom until you hear the roots crack, you've been building the kind of wrist strength that's right for arm wrestling. And judging by all the nickels spilling out of my can, I'm about to get handsomely *compensated,* as Mr. Khalil would say, for all the yard work I did.

Trouble is, this boy's arm is not going down easy. And the look in his eye says we've got some unfinished business to settle. I know what it is, too. He's still mad 'cause he thinks I disrespected his brother.

And I'm still mad 'cause he disrespected me.

My arm's got the advantage now. On the downward side of things—forty-five degrees if you know your geometry. But Leslie is cheering for Charlie Ross, and she's got eyes for him that must have some kind of magic. Potion eyes, I'd call 'em, because now our arms are standing straight up, like a soldier.

"Go, Charlie, go!" Magic Girl screams. My arm starts leaning the wrong way, like the soldier just got shot.

Charlie

Our two arms are trembling in a black and white blur. I can feel the big vein in my neck bulging out. Every muscle in my body is tight.

"Come on, Charlie, you can do it!"

"Take him down, Ross."

"Charlie, I'm rooting for you."

That's Leslie, whose sweet voice is a shot of adrenaline. Armstrong's arm is getting weaker. It's going down! I'm winning!

"Go, Ross, go! Go, Ross, go! Go, Ross, go!"

The whole school is cheering me on. Even Mr. Mitchell is watching from his upstairs window. And Mrs. Gaines from her corner on the yard. I've got the momentum. I've got the advantage. Soon I'll have a whole week's milk money, times forty kids.

"Charlie! Charlie! Charlie!"

Armstrong leans in. I can smell the peanut butter on his breath.

"Say, Ross," he says, his mouth inches from my ear. The veins in his neck are pulsing.

"What?" I grunt.

"Yo' mama's left titty callin'."

"Huh?"

"Yo' mama's left titty. It's callin' you for a drink of milk."

I can't help it. My vein-popping concentration gives way to a smile, which turns to a snort, which spreads to a giggle, which explodes to laughter. Soon I'm laughing so hard my arm goes limp.

And gets slammed onto the table, belly-up like a dead fish.

The bell rings. Armstrong grabs his tin can. Coins rain into his pockets. And he jingles off to class.

Armstrong

Ninth of December and I'm in the Christmas spirit. At lunchtime I open up my box, and there's more silver in there than Jim Hawkins found on Treasure Island.

Mrs. Gaines is flapping around the schoolyard like usual. But when she sees how my box shines, she lands right beside me.

"What have you got there, Armstrong?"

"Ho Hos, ma'am. Thirty-six of 'em. Barely fit in my lunch box."

"Where are they from?"

"Market near my house. Don't worry, Mrs. Gaines, they're paid for. My own money, too."

Her eyes bulge like the kind on a bath toy when tiny hands give it a squeeze.

"Would you like to have one?" I say.

I set one on the table in front of her. Her long red fingernail plucks at the tin foil and peels it back. She's got the same color lipstick as her nails. I watch her red lips come apart and —well, you'd expect a proper lady like Mrs. Gaines, Yard Supervisor and all, to take a proper lady-size bite. But now it's my eyes' turn to bug out, 'cause here comes the hungriest bite of Ho Ho you ever saw. Half gone in one chomp.

"Well?"

"I can guarantee one thing, Armstrong," she says soon as the other half's gone, "this is *not* the last Ho Ho that Edwina Gaines will consume."

She winks at me and smiles. *Smiles.* Man, this really must be Santa's food.

Pretty soon it goes around that I'm giving away Ho Hos. A whole lot of kids come running up to me.

"Hey, Armstrong, can I have one?" a fourth-grader asks.

"Sure," I say.

"Can I?" says a boy with shoes untied.

"If you drink your milk with it."

"I will."

He's so cute. Must be a kindergartner.

More and more little feet come running. More and more Ho Hos go. And then a terrible thing happens.

I have to say no to little kids.

"I'm so sorry, boys and girls," I say. "But there are only five more Ho Hos in Armstrong's box. And those I've got to save."

I carry the last five over to Ross's table and set them down. "Here you go, Ross," I say. "I am sorry that I stole from your lunch. I hope you will accept my apology and my Ho Hos. And, while you're in an accepting mood, I hope you don't mind some advice."

"What?" he says in a tone that says he *does* mind.

"Tomorrow when you come to school, bring the two boxes you worked for, plus these five I just gave you, and hand 'em out to those kids over there. After they eat 'em and nobody's mouth catches fire, your reputation around here will be restored."

Charlie

When I tell my dad how Armstrong turned our nickels into his Ho Hos, and how he saved both our reputations, Dad says, "I guess you're even now."

I guess we are.

· 7 ·

TWO HOLIDAYS

Charlie

ANDY LOVED HANUKKAH. He loved the smell of melting wax and the light that got brighter with each new candle, each new night. We'd sit on the living room floor and spin dreidels for gold coins that were really chocolate. Sometimes a dollar bill would flutter down from the sky and land in the pot. Mom said it must've come from God Himself because we were such good boys. When we were little, we believed her. When we were older, we pretended to.

There's been no Hanukkah this year. Mom didn't bring out the menorah, and I didn't mind. What's the point of spinning a dreidel alone?

But something tells me we shouldn't let Andy's favorite holiday just go by.

I slide open the door to our dish closet, go up on my tippy-toes, and pull down the menorah. It belonged to my great-grandfather, Zayde Moishe, who was a rabbi "in the old country," as Andy used to say.

I grab a box of colored candles left over from last year. Who knows if we've even got enough? Tonight's the last night and I'll need eight plus the shammes.

I tip over the box and count. There are nine.

Mom always went a little crazy with the presents. Dad would say, "Let the holiday be about light. And the sweetness of applesauce on latkes. The boys hardly need eight nights of gifts."

"Trinkets," Mom said. "That's all they get. A little something to open each night."

Hanukkah brought us our Nerf basketball hoop, every board game we ever played, our Hot Wheels, and the walkie-talkies we'd stay up late chatting on. Mom called them trinkets. They were our favorite toys.

Upstairs, I push open the door to Andy's room. I'm the only one who really comes in these days. Except for Lily once in a while to clean. And Mom once in a while to cry.

I put the menorah on the windowsill, fill it with candles, and strike a match. I'd feel silly saying the prayer out loud by myself, so I say it in my head.

Then I light the candles.

When the last one is lit, I put the shammes in the center holder. I stand back and watch the burst of light in my brother's window.

"Happy Hanukkah, Andy," I whisper.

The floor creaks behind me. I turn around, and there's Mom. She doesn't say anything, just looks at me. And at the menorah.

"It's the last night," I say.

Her arms reach around her like she's cold.

"I didn't buy you anything."

"I don't want anything."

I look away from her, back at the candles.

"Sit with me till they burn out?"

Mom doesn't answer.

I don't move until I hear the mattress frame squeak. Then I turn and sit beside her on the bed.

When Andy and I were little, like maybe four and five, Mom would take us on outings. We'd go downtown to the public library or to the original Farmers Market at Third and Fairfax. If there was a crowd, she'd walk between us and hold our hands. When she spotted something she didn't want us to miss, like a dog in a shopping cart or a tourist in a big Texas hat, she'd tell us in Yiddish to *kee-kois*. It meant "give a look."

Or she'd just squeeze our hands twice. One squeeze for each syllable of *kee-kois*. We'd answer back with a single squeeze to say, *We saw, we gave a look*.

The light from all nine candles is so bright you can see them double in the window. It looks like two menorahs:

eighteen candles. That's something I want Mom to notice. So I take her hand and squeeze it twice.

She doesn't squeeze back.

Armstrong

Most times when we go to church, I fall into a deep trance. My eyes stay open, but really I'm asleep. It's a trick passed down in the Le Rois family, from Daddy to Lenai to Cecily to Charmaine to the twins to me. "You can sleep all you want in church," Daddy says, "but don't let Mama catch you with your eyes closed."

Tonight, though, I'm having a hard time staying asleep. The preacher is talking about gratitude for the gifts we receive all year, not just on Christmas. Gift of life. Gift of family. Gift of friendship. I wonder if my daddy got ahold of his sermon and is preparing us for what's *not* going to be under the tree when we get home.

Turns out there *are* some presents waiting. It's tradition to unwrap them in order, oldest to youngest, so Daddy goes first. He says what he always says on Christmas Eve, what he's been saying every year since I came along.

"You already gave me six gifts, Gracie. I don't know if I can handle one more."

"You're not getting another of those," she says. Then she slides him a big wrapped box. "Open this instead."

It's a brand new toolbox, red metal with a solid latch. Two trays for screwdrivers and pliers and drill bits, and under that a big empty space for his hammer and his sander and his drill. No new tools, but a beautiful box just the same.

He kisses her and says, "Your turn, Mama."

The rule is only one present per person. But for Mama we all break the rule. Daddy bought her a new dress for the one night a month they go out. Lenai gives her coupons for homemade cookies, cakes, and other sweets that will be off-limits to everybody but her. Cecily made a drawing of Mama's hands. Charmaine made a foot-tall pad of paper, each sheet stamped with DON'T FORGET! She made it in print shop for all the reminder notes Mama leaves Daddy around the house. The twins each made her an earring in metal shop, so she's got a pair. And I give her something I made out of a stick of wood that Mr. Khalil taught me how to whittle.

"Is this a gift for me or for you?" she teases, holding up the back scratcher.

"Both," I say.

Now the sisters start in. Lenai opens the latest Isley Brothers album. Cecily unwraps a set of watercolor paints. Charmaine gets a new softball glove. Nika and Ebony get new slippers. They split the colors to make two mismatched pairs.

Finally it's my turn. Daddy slides a heavy box over to me. I rip through the Santas and the snowflakes and —

"What's this?" I ask.

"Your new lunch box."

"Looks like your old toolbox to me."

"Well . . . it'll keep your sandwich safe."

"Daddy," I say, "if I bring lunch to school in this thing, people will think I'm the maintenance man."

"Why don't you open it and see what's inside?"

I raise the latch and turn back the lid. The whole thing smells like rusty screws, chocolate, and something I can't identify because it's a new scent to my nose. I lift the tray and see a chocolate Santa from See's Candies. And under that a brand-new shirt, dark green with a light green collar. And the tag still on!

"For when you're not in the mood for pink," Daddy says. And we all bust up.

But the best gift of all is the knock at the door. When I invited old Mr. Khalil to join us at church, he said that he lacked the *posterior* for a night in the pews. "The wood," he explained, "in prolonged contact with my underside, is like bone on bone, Armstrong. If it were a wedding or a funeral, I could make it through. But if I sit for a Christmas Mass, I may never get up."

"How about afterward you come by our house for dinner? We've got plenty of cush on the couch."

"I couldn't leave Patches."

"He's welcome too, Mr. Khalil. It's Christmas."

Well, guess who just showed up with a bag of books for us all. Our very own Santa Claus. He even brought his dog.

That preacher was right. We've got a lot to be grateful for right here.

· 8 ·

SHADOW WORDS

Armstrong

IN THE MIDDLE OF JANUARY it starts to rain. Not the dib-
ble-dibble-dop kind you can run around in. This is a crack-
open-the-sky rain, with wind that flips umbrellas inside
out and puddles so deep your socks never dry. It rains so
much we're stuck inside for a whole week. Mrs. Valentine's
class is playing word games, holding story contests, and
learning how to square-dance. There's laughter and noise
and a whole lot of bumping up against our shared wall. It's
like the kids next door have a stash of sunshine all their
own.

Meantime, our class stays in the dark. Mr. Mitchell puts
on filmstrips and reads his *Los Angeles Times* by flashlight
while we're in a coma of atomic energy, oil refineries, and
the colonial era in American history. When the lights come
on, we get to do math exercises, spelling drills, and gram-
mar work sheets. By the fourth day our heads are dripping

with decimals and prepositional phrases, like those gutters are dripping with rain.

On day five, when the classroom feels like the hospital where my mama works, Mr. Mitchell brings out the record player.

"Today you're going to meet a great American song-writer," he says.

"Jim Morrison," somebody shouts.

"Joni Mitchell," says somebody else.

"Cat Stevens?" Shelley wonders.

"Stevie Wonder!" I say.

Mr. Mitchell wags his head at every guess.

He holds up an album cover, and I can see a white man with a straight nose and dark eyes and a banjo in his hand. "Stephen Foster," Mr. Mitchell says.

A stack of song sheets gets passed around the room, one for every table. Mr. Mitchell slides the record out of its sleeve and eases it onto the turntable. The disc starts to spin. The needle comes down and rides over scratches and dust. This must be a really old record.

Music fills the room. And I see Charlie Ross's face change like the tune brought him a memory.

Charlie

The voice on the record, like the words on the song sheets, sings:

> *Camptown ladies sing this song,*
> *Doo-dah! Doo-dah!*
> *Camptown racetrack's five miles long,*
> *Oh, doo-dah day!*

But in my head I'm singing the words me and Andy made up to this same tune:

> *Mammoth Mountain, here we come,*
> *Doo-dah! Doo-dah!*
> *Mammoth Mountain, here we come,*
> *Oh, doo-dah day!*

We're in the way way back of the station wagon, loaded up with winter clothes, snacks, board games, ski and after-ski boots, Andy, and me. My hand is pressed to the car window, the temperature dropping with each curve. Out that same window I see the shadows of four sets of skis pointing their tips up Highway 395, reaching for the mountain ahead. And just past those shadows, brightening the side of the road, is a bank of stark white snow. We're going skiing. All the doo-dah week long.

Dad always let us explore the mountain on our own. "As long as you ski on the buddy system," he said.

We liked the back of the mountain, over on chair 9. It was the longest ride and had the shortest lines. Each chair had a safety bar you could pull down, with a footrest for your skis.

On sunny days we'd kick back and work on our tans.

On snowy days we'd bundle up. Andy was the Masked Marvel in his facemask, goggles, and scarf. The harder it snowed, the louder he sang "Here Comes the Sun" by the Beatles.

Once I skied ricochet way too fast, caught an edge, and flipped over. I landed with my arms stuck in two feet of snow up to my shoulders.

I started to panic. Andy was there in a flash.

"Charlie," he said, "you okay?"

He lifted me out of the snow, cleaned my goggles with his lens cleaning paper, and helped me back into my skis.

"That's a little fast for this run," he said. "You should try it again when the light's better, and maybe take it slow next time."

The record crackles to the next song, and a woman's voice sings:

The sun shines bright in the old Kentucky home.
'Tis summer, the darkies are gay,

The corn top's ripe and the meadow's in the bloom
While the birds make music all the day.

It's one song sheet per table, so Armstrong and I share. During "Camptown Races" he was singing along, tapping the floor with his left foot and joining in.

He's not singing along now.

The time has come when the darkies have to part,
Then my old Kentucky home, good night!

The record spins. Two tables over, Shelley Berman is mouthing the words but not singing them. Then her mouth closes. Otis is slumped in his chair. Alex Levinson isn't singing. Armstrong's still not. And now neither am I.

Mr. Mitchell is walking around the room, adding his deep voice to the song.

The head must bow and the back will have to bend,
Wherever the darkey may go.
A few more days and the trouble all will end,
In the field where the sugar-canes may grow.

Mr. Mitchell stops behind our table and rests his hand on Armstrong's shoulder.

"How come you're not singing?"

Armstrong shrugs. Mr. Mitchell steps to his desk and

lifts the needle off the record. The room is silent except for the rain.

"Stephen Foster is a great American songwriter. He's part of our culture."

"He ain't a part of mine."

Mr. Mitchell comes back to our table.

"It's that word, isn't it?" he says, pointing to "darkies" on the song sheet. "He doesn't mean it in a bad way. Language is constantly changing, boys and girls. When Stephen Foster wrote 'My Old Kentucky Home,' the word *darkies* just meant black people. His lyrics actually gave them a new dignity they hadn't had before in song."

I glance at Armstrong. The look on his face is more like shame.

"If you don't feel like singing, Armstrong, you can just listen."

"Can I leave?"

"Excuse me?"

"Can I leave the class?"

Mr. Mitchell laughs. "Where would you go?"

"Outside in the hall. Until the song ends."

"And be unsupervised?"

"I'll just stand there. When it's over, I'll come back in."

Mr. Mitchell stares at Armstrong. Armstrong stares back. Then Mr. Mitchell sweeps his hand toward the door.

He puts the needle back down. The song starts over. He turns the volume way up.

Armstrong

. . .

Charlie

By lunchtime kids are splashing around in puddles and warming up in the sun. The yard is still wet, but I check out a sockball and declare myself captain of one team. Jason says he'll be captain of the other. He gets first pick and chooses Armstrong. I get next two and take Otis and Leslie—Otis because I want to win and Leslie because I want her to know she's my first pick. As the rest of the players get chosen, I notice Armstrong off to the side, bouncing the ball in a steady rhythm, his hand in a hammer fist.

Our team wins rock-paper-scissors, so we're up first. Otis comes to the plate and socks the ball through an opening between Armstrong and Alex. Jason runs it down, but by the time he throws it in from the outfield, Otis is standing calmly on second base.

Being captain gives me a chance to do what I've been waiting all year to do: whisper something, anything, into

Leslie's ear. So when it's her turn to be up, I tap her shoulder, lean close to her shiny black hair, and bring my lips within kissing — I mean, whispering — range.

"Bunt," I breathe.

She lifts her eyes toward mine and nods. It feels like a *yes* to a boy on one knee.

I don't know how, but Armstrong must've overheard. Because when Leslie lifts the ball with her left hand, Armstrong creeps forward from third base. And when she gives the ball a tiny tap, he's already racing toward it.

"Go, Leslie!" we shout from our bench. She runs like a gazelle, her feet slapping the wet ground. In sockball there are two ways you can get out: either the baseman catches a throw from the field before you step on the base, like in baseball; or you get hit by the ball, like in dodgeball.

Leslie is halfway to first when Armstrong fires. *Not* at the baseman.

Leslie limps home to our silent bench.

But her sacrifice brought Otis to third and me to the plate. I size up the outfield, see Shelley daydreaming in right, and —

BLAM! I smack that rubber ball so high that astronomers are about to discover a new planet.

Otis skips home while I round second. Jason covers for Shelley, fielding the ball after it bounces off the back fence. He throws it in to Armstrong just as I'm rounding third.

"Charlie, look out!" Leslie screams. The ball hurtles toward me at a speed faster than a meteor — the speed of Armstrong's right arm.

So I freeze. My untucked Wilson tennis shirt flaps in the wind as the ball whizzes by in a near miss. I skip the rest of the way home.

"OUT!" a voice roars from behind.

"Nice try, Armstrong," I say.

"That ball touched your shirt."

"Its breeze touched my shirt. The ball missed. The run's ours. Two nothing. One out."

"You're a damn liar."

"You're a sore loser."

"Come over here and say that to my face."

The last time we faced each other like this, I backed down out of fear. But I'm not about to this time. Some things are worth fighting for.

I turn around and walk right up to him.

"You're a sore loser," I say.

My hands form fists, just like my dad's did in the navy. Armstrong and I circle each other, boxers in the first round. If one steps forward, the other steps back. If one steps left, the other goes right.

The crowd rings us so fast it's like they were always there. And then I hear someone start to chant:

"Fight, fight! Darkey and a white!"

For half a second Armstrong's eyes leave mine to make a mental note of who said it first. But soon the chant gets taken up from behind him.

"Fight, fight! Darkey and a white!"

He jerks his head around to see who else said it.

The circle around us feels like a cage, the chant like a drum. "Fight! Fight!"

But in my head I hear a song. *The sun shines bright in the old Kentucky home* . . .

Suddenly I don't want to fight Armstrong anymore. It's Stephen Foster I want to fight. And Mr. Mitchell. And this crowd that won't stop shouting, "FIGHT! FIGHT! DARKEY AND A WHITE!"

Just then, a ball flies over my shoulder and bashes Armstrong on the head. He spins around and looks at me with rage in his eyes.

His fist flies up. It strikes me in the jaw.

My head whips back. Blood splatters the blacktop. Armstrong knees me in the gut. I try to breathe but there's ice in my chest. My feet get swept out from under me.

The fight is over. The white is on the ground.

INCIDENT REPORT

Submitted by: Edwina Gaines, Yard Supervisor at Wonderland Avenue School

Date of Incident: Friday, January 17, 1975

Time: 12:50 p.m.

Location: the lower yard

The children were playing sockball and Charlie Ross was rounding third when Armstrong threw him—well, that's just it—either he threw him out or he threw and missed and Charlie would have scored a run. The boys disagreed. There was loud shouting and insistence that each was correct. I drifted over, but soon a wall of other students enclosed them. Then a cry roared up from the crowd that went something like "Fight, fight!"—and then a word I don't care to put on paper—"and a white."

I blew my whistle and made my way through that wall of students. I discovered Charlie Ross on the ground, folded over with the wind knocked out of him. I gave him my full attention and, once he recovered, escorted both boys to the office of the principal.

Armstrong

"Here," I say, handing Ross a paper towel with a little red stain. "Your tooth."

We're side by side in the office, waiting for the secretary

to type Mrs. Gaines's Incident Report. Ross is trembling and I don't blame him for that. I know what it feels like to get the wind knocked out of you.

He looks at the paper towel. Doesn't take it, though.

"I saw it on the ground while Mrs. Gaines was tending to you. Since I'm the one who popped it out of your mouth, I'm the one should give it back."

I hold it out to him some more. He still doesn't take it.

"Might be worth something at home."

He won't look at me, but he takes the tooth and tucks it in his pocket. Snot trailing down his nose. Streams drying under his eyes. Here comes another shaky breath.

The thing is, I wasn't that mad at Ross. I was mad at whoever said that word. And at Stephen Foster for writing the song. And Mr. Mitchell for playing it. Everything got messed together. Though I still think Ross was out on my throw. And that was cheap, hurling a ball at my head when it was turned.

Man, I wish he would just breathe.

Sometimes one word's so hard to say. I can say it in my mind. *Sorry.* I can think up other words to go along with it. *Ross, believe me when I say I am sorry I knocked the wind out of you. And the tooth.*

But between the mind and the mouth is a long way.

"You all right?" I say.

No answer.

"I'll take that as a maybe. Look, Ross—"

"Shut up," he says. "I don't want to talk about it."

Looks like we won't be talking, then.

Charlie

In the principal's office Mrs. Wilson's glasses hang by that heavy chain. She sees me still trembling. I've got snot trails on my upper lip. My mouth tastes like blood.

She looks at Armstrong, perfectly calm. Could he be scared? I hope he's scared.

"Sit down, boys."

We sit. She hands me a tissue from the box on her desk. I blow my nose as quietly as I can.

"The punishment for starting a fight at Wonderland," she says, "is expulsion from the school."

Armstrong looks right at her. "Send me back, then, if that's your rule."

They stare at each other. Mrs. Wilson sighs, leans back, and looks at us both.

"Do you boys know why Wonderland is an Opportunity Busing school? I requested it. I asked to be part of this experimental year. You should have seen the mob of parents in here. What's wrong with Wonderland the way it is, they said. A neighborhood school. A strong community. Kids who've grown up together. Why bring in another element? This is Laurel Canyon, they said. Not Little Rock. Not Boston. Exactly, I told them. It's Laurel Canyon. Where everyone can learn to get along."

She looks at Armstrong. "Was I mistaken?"

He looks away.

"I've read Mrs. Gaines's report. I know that a hurtful word was chanted on the yard. It can't have been easy for you to hear, Armstrong. But physical violence is never acceptable at this school. You made a boy bleed. You put him on the ground. A kid who reacts like that . . ."

She's really going to kick him out. If I don't say anything, Armstrong'll be gone for good. I'll never have to deal with him again.

Just as wrong to ignore an injustice, Charlie . . .

My dad's voice in my head. But what about *my* voice? The one that couldn't talk twenty minutes ago because I couldn't breathe?

Just as wrong . . .

I look at Armstrong, at Mrs. Wilson, at Armstrong again. Then I say the words. Not loud. But I say them.

"He didn't start the fight."

"What's that, Charlie?"

"Armstrong didn't start the fight."

"He threw the first punch. That's what the witnesses said. It's here in the report."

"Only after somebody threw a ball at his head."

Armstrong snaps his head my way. I can feel his anger rising.

"Why say 'somebody' when you know it was you?"

"It wasn't me. It came from behind. I don't know who threw it."

"For real?"

"For real."

"Honestly," Mrs. Wilson says, "I don't see how it matters where the ball came from. What matters is your reaction, Armstrong. End of story."

But it's not the end of the story, I think. There's another part that wasn't in Mrs. Gaines's report.

"The word didn't come from the school yard," I say. "It came from class. From a song Mr. Mitchell played. It upset Armstrong. He asked to leave the room."

"What was the song?"

"'My Old Kentucky Home.'"

Her eyes close. She lifts her glasses to her mouth and bites down on the frame. She sits there thinking for so long that the clock does its backwards *tick* and its forward *tock* as a whole minute goes by.

"Well," Mrs. Wilson finally says, "I can't exactly expel a song."

Under her breath, I think I hear her say, *Or a teacher.* But I'm not really sure.

• • •

We come out of the office, and I get a drink of water from the fountain. It's a long fountain with three faucets so more than one kid can drink at a time.

Armstrong steps up and turns the knob on the last spout. I drink at my end. He drinks at his.

Armstrong

"I'm surprised you lasted this long," Mama says when she tucks me in.

"Aren't you going to ask what happened?"

"You lost your temper, I suppose."

"Aren't you going to ask why?"

She doesn't. But I tell her anyway. I've got to so she'll know it was different this time.

Afterward she sighs and says, "He *had* to pick that song."

"He said language is changing all the time. And Stephen Foster didn't mean any harm. But it felt like harm to me. So I asked could I leave the room."

"You left the room?"

"Old Mr. Khalil says to be who I am, not who they expect me to be. Mr. Mitchell expected me to just sit there and listen. But that's not who I am."

"You did the right thing, Armstrong."

"The anger came out later, during a game. And then

somebody—I didn't see who—called me the word from the song. Only it wasn't just one somebody, Mama, but a whole crowd. The whole school, it felt like."

You can hear the train whistle from over by the tracks. Most nights that's the sound I fall asleep to. We wait for the train to pass.

Then Mama says, "You know, Armstrong, this program, it's not mandatory. If you have to, if you *want* to, you can go back to Holmes anytime."

I don't answer right away. I got to think about that.

"A funny thing is," I say, "Charlie Ross—that's the boy I got in a fight with—he told the truth. All of it." I got my cheek on the pillow, so I can't see Mama's face. But I can picture the wrinkles that show up every time she's lost in thought.

"Scratch my back?"

The covers come down. My shirt lifts up. Here come her nails, light and soft, the way I like it.

"I wish I could tell you that's the last time you'll hear that word," she says.

"I know."

"Or others, even worse."

"I know."

"They're our shadow words."

She scratches some more.

"You think his people got a shadow word?"

"What do you mean, 'his people'?"

"Back in September, Charlie Ross was out of school for

one day. Ten days later, he was out for another. Said his mama made him go to temple."

"That means they're Jewish. Yes, they have a shadow word."

"You know what it is?"

"I do. But you don't need to."

Charlie

The Tooth Fairy catches me tucking my tooth under my pillow. She wants to know what happened.

"Armstrong and I got in a fight. It didn't last long. One punch was all it took."

"What precipitated the fight?" the Tooth Fairy's husband wants to know.

I tell them about the song and the game and the chant. I tell them I'm glad I don't have to lift weights anymore or stand up to Armstrong in front of the school, because now everyone knows I'm a wuss who could never kick his ass anyway, so why try?

"Is there anything we can do for you?" Dad says.

"Yeah," I say. "I'd like fifty cents for my tooth so I can buy some candy from the Helms Man."

"Look under your pillow tomorrow. Is there anything else?"

There *is* something else. Something I thought of when

we were in Mrs. Wilson's office and she almost threw Armstrong out of school.

"I want to go to Carpenter with Keith. Can we use Aunt Trudy's address in Studio City so I don't have to go back to Wonderland?"

There's a long silence while Mom and Dad just look at each other. Sometimes parents can look at each other for only a few seconds and have, like, a twenty-minute conversation.

"We're not going to do that, Charlie," my dad says.

"Why not? Why can't we be like the other families? There are no Armstrongs at their schools."

"Because we're not like those other families. We don't run away from problems. We deal with them."

I turn away to the wall. All I want to do is sleep.

· 9 ·

ONE SATURDAY

Charlie

"Two for flinching."

It's a Saturday morning in February, and I feel the double tap of a fist on my shoulder. I turn around and see Keith standing on our driveway. I just finished washing my mom's car and would've seen him coming, but I was coiling up the hose.

"Hey, Keith," I say. "How's it going?"

"One boring day at a time," he says. "Wanna make this one stand out?"

Before his parents pulled him out of Wonderland, Keith was the one kid I wanted to be able to call my best friend. He's fearless, a tiny bit crazy, and fun. He gets me to take risks I'd never take on my own.

"What do you want to do?"

"Ride our bikes down to Studio City."

In the category of unintentional injuries, car accidents

are the deadliest kind. Next comes drowning, and after that, other transportation.

Including bikes.

To get to Studio City, you have to ride along Mulholland Drive. It's a twisty road on the top of a mountain. One pothole and you could go over the edge. If that's not dangerous enough, then comes the deathtrap of Laurel Canyon Boulevard. Four lanes. Speeding cars. A whole lot of steep.

"How will we get home?"

"Easy. My mom'll pick us up. We'll tell her *your* mom drove us down with our bikes in her trunk so we could ride around in the flats where it's safe. Our moms don't talk much anymore, so we'll trick 'em both."

Keith sees me hesitating.

"That was Andy's, wasn't it?" he says, pointing to the Mammoth Mountain sweatshirt I'm wearing.

"Yeah."

"We can go to Baskin-Robbins and get ice cream. We'll drink a couple of malts in his honor. Jamoca Almond Fudge. That was his favorite, right?"

He remembers.

"And I'll show you my new school."

"I don't know, Keith," I say. "You think it's safe?"

"I don't know, Charlie Ross," he says. "You think it's safe?"

His blue eyes laser through me.

Armstrong

Having all sisters, and all of them older, is its own kind of education. For instance, I'll bet you Ross doesn't know there's a right way and a wrong way to dry their *personal items*. You have to hang them on the line for the whole neighborhood to see. If you dry them in the machine, they stretch.

"Armstrong, bring in the laundry. It's hanging on the line."

"Can't my sisters do it? It's mostly their underthings out there."

"Which is why," my daddy says, "they're not about to step outside without 'em."

So here I am, snatching bras off the line and praying none of the boys around here see me. But here comes Jerome and his let's-laugh-at-Armstrong smile. And here's me in plain sight with three bras and six panties draped over my arms. Fourth bra around my neck, like a scarf.

"Say, Armstrong, if you get tired of wearing your sisters' clothes, I got some old ones you can have."

"These aren't my sisters' clothes," I say.

"They're not?"

"They belong to my girlfriend."

"You got a girlfriend with cups that size?"

"I'm going with a college girl."

"Armstrong, you ain't dating no college girl."

"As a matter of fact, I am."

"What's her name?"

"Beatrix."

"Beatrix what?"

"Potter. She goes to USC. Majoring in reverse psychology."

"For real?"

I look Jerome straight in the eye without even a twitch. Reach up and pluck Charmaine's panties off the line. "Jerome," I say, "do you know what the word *entrepreneur* means?"

"No."

"Are you familiar with the work of Mr. James Emanuel?"

"I'm familiar with the work of Mr. James Brown."

"I am referring to the poet, not the singer. Or the running back."

"Never heard of him."

"Well, maybe if you dated a *college* girl like Beatrix Potter, you'd expand your horizons like I'm expanding mine. Now, if you don't mind, Beatrix is waiting for her bras."

I carry that laundry inside and put the shade down. I don't want Jerome looking for Beatrix in my window.

And I don't want him seeing my five sisters in search of their clothes on a Saturday morning. I just stand there like a hat rack and let them pluck what they need.

A bra gets snatched off my neck.

"Thanks, Armstrong," Lenai says.

"Those are mine!" Ebony says, yanking some panties off my left arm.

"They're mine!" Nika says. "You bought the yellow ones, remember?"

They go on fighting over the pair. Charmaine and Cecily come for their things, and pretty soon I'm empty.

In case you were wondering, I kept my eyes closed the whole time. They're my sisters!

Charlie

On Skyline Drive we pop wheelies onto a vacant lot, one of about twenty-five that tumble like a giant set of stairs down to Mulholland Drive. Soon they'll have construction sites for us to play on. But for now the empty lots are where we ride.

"Race you."

There's no "ready, set, go." We fly over the first lip, land on the next lot, and tear across it, Keith on his Stingray in the lead. I beat him across the next few lots, but just before the last one he surges ahead, skidding to a dusty stop ahead of me.

We ride Mulholland single file, Keith out front, me hugging the edge. A car buzzes by on my left. My front wheel wobbles. I veer close to the cliff. But at the last second I regain control.

At Laurel Canyon the light is red. I catch up to Keith. Side by side we wait for the green.

"So, Charlie Ross, you kick the black kid's ass yet?"

"Who, Armstrong?"

"According to Leslie, he kicked yours."

"You talked to Leslie?"

"She's in Girl Guides with my sister. Said you got in a fight, but he beat you real fast. Know what I think?"

I look up at Keith.

"Promise you won't get mad."

"I promise."

"You lost your confidence when Andy died. I'm going to help you build it back up." The light turns green. "You with me?"

I nod, but I'm not sure.

"Let's boogie!"

Keith dashes ahead into a left turn. I pump hard to catch up.

Laurel Canyon gets real steep real fast. I step on my brakes going downhill, then ease up on them just to see if I can. My stomach flips as we gather speed. Keith is up on his pedals now, high over his banana seat, T-shirt flapping in the wind.

What if something goes wrong right now? What if a car swings wide on a turn or skids and knocks me off the bike? I could be dead in an instant. But that can't happen, can it? Two brothers in one family? That's like lightning striking twice in the same place. No—Andy used up all our bad luck. I'm safe. Now and forever.

I stand up on my pedals the way Keith did. Woo-hoo! Look who's *traveling* now, Armstrong!

Armstrong

I tried to get some of the boys around here to work for me. But nobody wanted a job. I didn't know where to find some good labor to help with my business, which I call Armstrong's Odds & Ends.

But this morning, with my eyes closed and panties getting plucked from my arms, I realized I've got a pool of labor right here.

My sisters!

Charmaine says she's too busy on a Saturday (never says doing what), but Nika and Ebony offer to pull weeds for a dollar a yard.

"Fifty cents each?" I said.

"A dollar each."

Trouble is, I already told Mr. Wong, who runs the corner store, that I'd weed his yard for two fifty. Which means I'll be making a profit of only fifty cents a yard.

On the other hand, they're my sisters.

On the other *other* hand, I'm running a business here.

"Fine," I told them. "Seventy-five cents *each* a yard."

"A dollar!"

"Okay, a dollar." At least it stays in the family.

I put Cecily to work painting a mural for Mrs. Roland. She lives up the street from Mr. Khalil and is tired of staring at concrete. I'll pay my sister good money too. Five dollars for a whole wall. (Mrs. Roland promised me ten.) Lenai asked what she could do, and I said one of my clients, Mrs. Croft, has a south-facing yard that gets enough sun for a vegetable garden. Lenai's got the soil all churned up and ready to plant when, about ten o'clock, I drop by with packets of seeds.

"Aren't you going to help me plant them?" Lenai says.

"I'll be back just as soon as I drop off this paint for Cecily up the street."

I also got to check on Nika and Ebony to make sure they're twisting until they hear the roots crack.

It's a lot of work organizing so many jobs.

Charlie

At Vantage Avenue, Keith makes a left in front of an oncoming car. The driver honks, and Keith flips him the bird. I try to flip him the bird too, but my middle finger doesn't point straight like Keith's. His shoots out like an arrow. Mine's more like limp Play-Doh.

For breakfast we have Baskin-Robbins. "Two Jamoca

Almond Fudge malts," Keith tells the girl behind the counter. He says it's his treat, to pay me back for those Razzles. We drink our malts in Buddy Brown's Toy Store next door.

Where Keith sees me eyeing a Whirly Wheel.

"Gonna buy it?"

I finger the ten dollars I *borrowed* from my mom's purse.

"Too expensive," I say.

"They're having a special today. It's free."

"It is?"

"If you move fast enough. I'll create a diversion. You snatch and run. We'll meet in front of the movie theater."

Keith walks up to the cash register with a pack of baseball cards. The manager rings him up, and the next thing I know, Keith is projectile vomiting his Jamoca Almond Fudge malt into the open register! He doubles over, clutching his belly, then stands up and sprays more half-digested malt at the manager's tie.

This is my chance to swipe the Whirly Wheel and run. I grab it from the shelf, glance over at the register, and see the manager handing Keith a towel. All I have to do is turn and walk out the back door.

Which I do.

After putting the Whirly Wheel back on the shelf.

We meet up by the movie theater down the block. Keith falls against me, hysterically laughing. He slams me into the ticket booth.

"That right there was totally bitchin'. Know what he said to me? *Are you okay, young man? Would you like me to call your mom?*" Keith laughs some more. Then he looks at me and says, "Where's the Whirly Wheel?"

I don't answer right away. I get a twisty feeling in my stomach.

"Charlie? Where's the Whirly Wheel?"

"Still in the store."

"What?"

I look down at Keith's shirt. At the brown stain.

"But I set you up," he says.

"I'm sorry, Keith. It just felt wrong to me."

He looks at me, through me, with those icy blue eyes. Then he smiles and says it's okay. "To get your confidence back," he says, "it can take more than one try."

Armstrong

I cut across the park, and that's when I find out why Charmaine didn't want to work for me. She's with her boyfriend, Lester Davies, smooching by the swings. Daddy would kill her if he knew. He's been out of the army since the end of the Korean War, but when it comes to my sisters, he's Sergeant Theodore Le Rois all over again. His mission: keep them safe from what he calls "enemy advances." You can tell who the enemy is by the uniform: tank top, jeans, a baseball cap, and a patch of fuzz on the upper lip. In other words, teenage boy. When my daddy sees one coming, he gives them a look that would make any soldier retreat. And if they dare launch some ammo at the house—a box of candy or a record album or, if they're crazy, some flowers—he orders them to "STAY AWAY FROM MY GIRLS UNTIL YOU'VE GOT A DIPLOMA!"

Lester dropped out of high school. That's why they meet here at the park, out of range of the sergeant's binoculars.

Charlie

The playground at Carpenter has four handball courts to our one, a full basketball court, and the painted oval lines of a track. I try to imagine playing sockball on a field this big. I'll bet even Armstrong can't clear the fence.

We ride around to the back of the school and park our bikes. In the far corner there's a gap in the gate just big enough for us to slide under. Keith leads me over to a building. He boosts me up to the window so that I can see into his classroom. He knows exactly where everything is, even without looking.

"See that poster of the presidents," he says, "on the wall opposite the clock?"

It's a banner with mostly lame sketches of all the U.S. presidents, from Washington to Ford. "I did the one of Nixon," Keith tells me. "My dad says we're going to miss him. One of the best presidents we've ever had."

Instead of telling Keith what *my* dad says about Nixon, I ask, "Where do you sit?"

"From the teacher's desk, four rows back and two seats in. You remember who sits right in front of me, don't you?"

I picture a foxy blonde with hair that smells like rain. That's when several pebbles whistle past my ear and plink off the window. Keith drops me like a brick, and we spin around. Three kids—two boys in jeans and a girl in a halter-top—face us.

"Busted, man," the taller and tougher of the two boys says.

"Lucky it's by you." Keith play-punches him in the arm, then introduces me as a friend from his neighborhood.

"Charlie Ross, say hello to Tim and Randy."

Tim is a tough-looking kid, with long feathered hair and dark eyes. Randy is about my height, but his hair looks like it was buzzed by an army barber. He wears a T-shirt with a cow drawn on the front and the word "COWSHIRT" under it. But he safety-pinned a crease over the *R*.

"And this," Keith says, tugging the strap on the girl's overalls, "is Jodie St. Claire."

I already smelled that.

"We're heading over to Fryman Canyon," Tim says. "Tons of lizards over there. Wanna come?"

"Sure we'll come," Keith says.

Then Randy asks me if I know how to catch a lizard. That's like asking a Montana boy if he knows how to catch a fish. The only Laurel Canyon kids who can't catch lizards are total wusses. At first sight of a lizard, guys like Keith and Tim and Randy stick out a hand to stop the foot traffic behind them. They know how to tell a horned toad from a blue-belly, how to tie a slipknot, and how to make a noose out of reed.

At first sight of a lizard, my hand reacts just as fast. It reaches down and grabs on to my privates. Don't ask me why. When I'm scared—really, really scared—that's just where my hand goes.

My herpetophobia is so great that I've rehearsed socially acceptable excuses in case someone asks me if I want to touch one.

Nah, I've got a bunch at home I can hold.

No, thanks—you look like you could use the practice.

That's okay, I've got a skin disease. The doctor says it's contagious to reptiles.

So when Randy asks me if I know how to catch a lizard, I say, "Sure—don't you?"

"Well, since you're on our turf, it's only right you get the first catch."

From Carpenter, the trailhead to Fryman Canyon is a

short bike ride up Laurel Canyon, then right on Fryman. I don't know my way around here, so I bring up the rear. Jodie St. Claire hangs back and waits for me.

"So you go to Wonderland?"

"Yeah."

"I hear black kids get bused to that school."

"A few."

"I hear they steal."

"You ever steal anything?" I ask.

"Just candy and lipstick and stuff."

"Sometimes I take coins from my mom's purse," I say. "To buy candy."

"The nice thing about stealing candy," Jodie says, "is you swallow the guilt."

We ride on a bit, both of us trying to think of something to say. She thinks faster.

"So, Charlie, you like lizards?"

"I like to leave them alone."

"Because . . . ?"

"I want them to leave me alone."

"You're scared of them."

"No. Course not. Well, maybe a little. But if you tell the guys, I'll kill you."

Jodie slides her thumb and finger across her lips, zippering them shut.

We look up and see Keith's hand pushed back to stop us

in our tracks. He's spotted a pair of blue-bellies, a larger one chasing a smaller one into the shadow of a rock. We all get off our bikes. The hunt is on.

Keith crouches out of the sun. Tim pitches a handful of dirt behind the rock. The two lizards run into the open and then freeze. Keith waves me over, and I creep toward him the way you sneak up on a brother or sister you're planning to scare. Soon I'm close enough to grab one of the lizards. My hand inches out. The smaller lizard gets away, but at the last second I slide my hands together, trapping the larger one. It starts to wriggle out of my grasp. I pinch its tail.

"Grab him by the belly!" Keith says. But just then the lizard jerks and squirms and gets away.

I look down at the detached tail between my fingers. It twitches like it's still getting signals from a brain. I toss it into the dirt.

The rest of the lizard has run into an ambush of boys. Keith dangles a looped reed in the air a few feet ahead. Tim flicks a pebble at the lizard; it darts into Keith's noose. Keith raises the reptile into the air, its mouth opening and closing, but with nothing to bite.

Randy holds out a plastic baggie with holes poked in it for air. Keith drops the lizard in, then turns to me.

"It's not a rat, Charlie Ross. You don't catch him by the tail."

As we walk away, I glance at the tail in the dirt. It's the first thing I've stolen today. I wish I could give it back.

Armstrong

After I leave paint for Cecily and check on Nika and Ebony and help Lenai get those seeds into the ground, I stop by Mr. Khalil's to see how he's getting along. He's getting along just fine—halfway up his old wooden ladder, this time against the side of his house.

"Mr. Khalil," I say, "what in the world are you doing halfway up a ladder?"

"Caulking my windows in advance of the next storm. The last one brought three inches of rain. Two of them wound up in my bedroom."

"That doesn't look safe to me."

"You think a man in his tenth decade isn't fit to climb a ladder?"

"No, I don't."

"Who's going to climb it for me?"

"I will."

"I can't pay you, Armstrong. I told you that."

"You already did pay me, Mr. Khalil. I'm making seven dollars today off my sisters. But if you want, you can teach me how to caulk a window."

Mr. Khalil looks down at me like I'm twenty feet beneath him, instead of two.

"It's an advanced skill," he says.

"Aw, come on, Mr. Khalil, you know I'm capable of this

kind of work. You can go inside your bedroom and coach me. That way I can add it to my *repertoire*."

He thinks about this, then climbs on down and hands me the caulking gun. "It takes a steady hand," he says. "Squeeze and sweep. Squeeze and sweep."

He shows me how.

Now with me on the ladder and Mr. Khalil inside his bedroom, we're just about eye to eye. I point the caulking gun at the groove between the glass and the window frame. I squeeze, but nothing comes out. I squeeze a little harder. It's like the gun is jammed. So I bang it on the edge of the ladder, and the next time I squeeze, a blob of gel goes splat against the window, blurring everything.

Mr. Khalil kneels down to a clear spot in the window, where he can see me. He motions for me to try again. I do, and this time the gun works right. I make a clean line of gel in the groove, and when I see that it's good, I ask Mr. Khalil what's been on my mind since I first met him.

"Were you ever married, Mr. Khalil?"

"Three times, Armstrong."

"Three?"

"You forget how old I am."

"What happened to your wives?"

And then, to pass the caulking time, Mr. Khalil tells me about all three of his wives.

The first was Tilly, his high school sweetheart. She wanted to start a family right away. *How are we going to support a family,* Mr. Khalil asked her, and she said, *You're healthy—get a job.* His job, he told her, was going to college, and she should be doing the same. But she didn't want to go to college, didn't want to wait four years to get a baby, so she found somebody else. Then Mr. Khalil met a girl on the train coming home from Michigan, after he got his first degree. They fell in love so fast, they were engaged by the time the train reached Atlanta, where he was headed to bury his grandma.

"So were you a daddy?"

"Almost," he says. "I lost both Althea and our son in childbirth."

The caulking gel goes on clear as a drop of clean water. I can picture the young Mr. Khalil standing over a hospital bed looking at his wife and their baby, neither one of them alive. I don't know what to say, or if there's anything to say. So I just go on caulking.

It's Mr. Khalil who starts the conversation again. He tells me it was a long time between his second wife and his third. She was the librarian at the high school where he taught English. Every time he checked out a book, he'd return it with a little note in the pocket where the card is supposed to go.

"You must've checked out a lot of books."

"Sometimes three in a week."

"What happened to her?"

"Cora died of cancer a year after we were married."

With all these sad stories coming from his side of the window, I feel like maybe I should share one from mine.

"I almost had a brother," I tell him. "He would've been nine years old now if he had lived past birth. Sometimes I pretend he's still alive. Make up stories to tell him. Games to play."

"That would have been one lucky boy, Armstrong."

Two lucky boys, I think.

Charlie

"True or false: lizards can swim."

Keith holds the bag over the swimming pool in Randy's backyard.

"True," I guess.

Keith unzips the bag and turns it over. The lizard slides out and swims along the surface, his head just above the water. With only a stump for a tail, he seems to have a hard time floating. But his body jerks from side to side, and his tiny legs paddle to keep him from going under.

Randy walks out of the house with Cokes for everyone. Keith sits on the lounge chair next to me, leans back, and crosses his legs like someone much older. He takes a swallow of Coke and then claps me on the shoulder.

"Me and the guys have decided to invite you in."

"In what?"

"Our club."

"Thanks, Keith. That's really nice of you."

"You're welcome, Charlie Ross. There's just one thing you gotta do."

"Yeah?"

"Something important. Something big enough to show that you're with us."

The pool pump buzzes like an old refrigerator. Randy comes through the door of the shed carrying a long aluminum pole with a net on one end. He kicks the door closed. The pump quiets down.

Tim sits at a table reading the comics.

"I got a live one!" Randy whoops. He holds the net out high, pretending he's caught a shark or something, but it's just the lizard in there. He holds it over Jodie's head. Pool water drips down her neck. She gives Randy a BB-eyed look.

"Let the lizard go," she says.

Tim turns to Keith. "Your girl's got a bad attitude. Tell her to leave."

"I'm nobody's girl. And I'm leaving because you guys are gross."

She gets up from the chair and looks at me.

"Charlie?"

My name on her lips. She's asking me to go with her because she knows I'm afraid of lizards, knows the last thing I want to do is hurt one.

What she doesn't know is how much I look up to Keith and want to be in his club.

The gate latch clicks behind her.

"We don't want a girl to see this anyway," Keith says. He tears off three sheets of the newspaper — the comics and a few pages of the classifieds. I catch a glimpse of Jughead and Veronica from the *Archie* strip.

Keith spreads out the pages on the table and says, "Roll up the comics, Charlie Ross, into a big cone."

I grab hold of Archie's arm and start rolling. Soon I'm holding a cone.

"Twist the bottom shut."

I do.

Keith turns to Randy and Tim.

"True or false: lizards can read."

Randy nods. "He's a pretty smart lizard. I say true."

"Drop him in and let's find out."

Randy holds the net six inches above the paper cone in my hand. With a swift jerk of his wrist, he tips it over and shakes the lizard out of the net and into the cone. There's a wild scratching sound, like tree branches at a window in a storm.

"False," says Keith.

"How do you know?"

"He's not laughing at the comics."

But we are at the joke.

"True or false: lizards can scream."

Nobody answers.

"Charlie?"

"I don't know."

Keith pulls out his pocketknife and a wrinkled book of matches. He uses the knife to widen the hole in a Coke can. Then he slides the matches across the table to me.

I feel dizzy and confused. Is he asking me to set the lizard on fire?

"This is how you build confidence, Charlie Ross. You walk right into your biggest fear . . . and out the other side."

Keith takes the cone from my hand.

"Go on. Light a match."

I pick up the book of matches, fold back the cover, and peel one off. I strike the match. It goes out in my trembling hand.

I strike another. The lizard scurries up the cone, looking for a way out. Keith shakes it back down. The boys are waiting, watching me. I'm watching the flame, wondering what'll happen if I do nothing. After six seconds or so, the flame will burn out. The people who made the matches planned it that way so your finger won't get burned. But it also gives you time to decide if you really want to light a fire. You've got those six seconds to change your mind.

The flame is creeping toward my finger, and I can feel its heat. I can feel the heat from the boys, too. They're waiting for me to set the lizard on fire. True or false, they want to know, is Charlie Ross a wuss, or one of us?

The match goes out in my hand.

"Give me the frickin' matches," Tim says. "I'll do it."

"No," I say. "I will."

I strike a third match.

"True or false," I say. "Lizards can scream."

The boys watch as I touch the burning match to the newspaper cone. The edge blackens, then curls into flame. The lizard scuttles up the side of the paper, and Keith shakes the lizard down one last time before setting the cone into the empty can.

We stand back and watch the comics burn.

True or false: lizards can scream.

False. They can't.

Halfway through dinner, the phone rings. Mom answers, and here's what I hear:

"This is the Ross residence, yes . . . You did? . . . Where? . . . Are you sure? . . . Which Mr. Ross? Oh, I see. What time? Really? Yes, we'll be by to pick it up tomorrow. Thank you for calling."

She puts down the phone and looks straight at me.

"What was that about?" my father asks.

"That was a man who lives on Laurel Canyon Boulevard. He was getting his mail this afternoon when he found a wallet in the gutter by his house. The ID card says it belongs to Mr. Ross."

My dad reaches down and checks his back pocket.

"My wallet's right here," he says.

"Mr. *Charlie* Ross."

I get a tight feeling in my belly. Probably how that lizard felt when Keith caught him.

In the garage, Dad hoists my bike up to the rafters with a rope. He ties the loose end of the rope to a hook on the wall. He knots it. He *triple* knots it. The bike swings from that rope like a convict.

"You see where your bike is hanging now?"

"Yes."

"That's where it's going to stay for a while."

"Until next week?"

"Longer than that."

"Next month?"

"You put yourself at great risk today. Once again you used poor judgment. Mulholland Drive, with those blind curves? Laurel Canyon? No sidewalks. Speeding cars. That *hill!* You could have been killed, Charlie."

I bow my head. "I guess I wasn't thinking," I say.

"Well, with your bike off-limits, you'll have plenty of time to think now."

"Until spring break?"

"Until you've earned it back by working for ten Saturdays at Ross Rents."

I turn and walk out of that garage. I don't want my father to see me cry.

· 10 ·

ARMSTRONG IN THE HOUSE

Charlie

ON THE DAY MRS. WILSON visits our classroom, even Mr. Mitchell sits up straight in his chair. It's the twenty-fourth of February, and the black-haired no-nonsense principal of Wonderland Avenue School interrupts our math drills to make an announcement: "The sixth-graders are going on a field trip."

Field trips are cool. Field trips give us a half day off from Mr. Mitchell's prison. They give us a ride on the long kind of school bus, an excuse to sing "Ninety-nine Bottles of Beer," and a chance to bounce around in the back seats. Sometimes the buses take us to interesting places, too. We've been on a tour of the *Los Angeles Times,* where the news gets cast in rubber and mounted on a giant drum that looks like a ditto machine. We've been to the La Brea Tar Pits, where thousands of years ago woolly mammoths, dire wolves, saber-toothed cats, and even a human—the La Brea Woman—were trapped in pools of oozing asphalt. We got to go whale watching once, but I took Dramamine and slept through the whole cruise.

Where will the sixty-seat Crown bus take us this time? The Descanso Gardens? The Huntington Library? The Los Angeles Zoo?

"You'll be gone a whole week," Mrs. Wilson says. "Saturday to Friday." In every row eyes and mouths open wide. Heads spin around. Voices rumble through the room.

Mrs. Wilson raises her hand for silence. "There's a science camp in the Angeles National Forest. Every week during the school year, two schools are selected for a weeklong visit to the Clear Creek Outdoor Education Center. This year it's Wonderland's turn."

The class cheers. Mrs. Wilson's hand comes up again for silence. She passes around a flyer and offers more details. "You'll need to pack your own bedding, warm clothes, and toiletries. Your meals will be provided by the camp's cafeteria. I expect you all, as ambassadors of our school, to be on your absolute best behavior.

"The bus will leave from Wonderland early Saturday morning and return the following Friday in time for the afternoon buses home," Mrs. Wilson continues. "But I need to ask your help for something. The regular school buses don't run on the weekends, and not all of our new families this year have cars. So we're looking for volunteers to invite Otis and Armstrong, and also Alma and Dezzy from Mrs. Valentine's class, to spend Friday night in your house before the field trip. That way they'll already be here in the Canyon for the early Saturday departure. Ask your parents, please, if they might be able to accommodate a guest for a sleepover that night."

The room is quiet. Armstrong and Otis look at their laps.

"Are there any questions?"

There are thousands. *Can we bring cameras? What if we don't like the food? Is it cold enough up there to see your breath in the mornings? Do the showers have doors? I still sleep with a stuffed animal; should I leave him at home?*

What if nobody volunteers?

But no one asks these questions out loud.

At last, one hand goes up in back. "Mrs. Wilson?"

We all turn around and look at Alex Levinson as he says, "Otis is my friend. I'll ask my mom if he can stay with us Friday night."

"Thank you, Alex."

She looks around the room. Is it for a second volunteer?

Shelley raises her hand. "Alma can sleep at my house."

"Thank you, Shelley. Make sure it's fine with your parents."

Mrs. Wilson waits a little more. When no more hands go up, she quietly leaves the room.

Armstrong

"I don't want to go on some school trip anyway," I tell my family that night at dinner.

There's a heavy rainstorm on. You can hear it doing a drum dance on the gutters.

"I'll go for you," Charmaine says.

"You can't go. You're a girl."

"We've got practically the same face."

"You going to cut your hair and start wearing *my* clothes? All for a stupid science camp?"

"He doesn't want to go because none of the kids invited him to stay over on Friday night," Lenai says.

"Is that right, Armstrong?" Mama asks.

I let my shoulder answer for me.

"Son," my daddy says, like he's all experienced in these matters, "just because nobody volunteered on the first day doesn't mean they won't on the second. You've got to give them a chance to go home and ask their families. That's the proper way to do things."

"Alex Levinson put his hand up for Otis."

"Guess you shouldn't have kicked that white boy's ass, then," Ebony says.

Charlie

Whoever said girls can't run faster than boys never got chased by Shelley Berman. She chases me around the schoolyard faster than a tetherball goes around a pole. The only thing that slows this girl down is the sign on the boys' bathroom, which is where I'm hiding now, just to catch my breath.

Mrs. Gaines, on the other hand, barges right in.

"Charlie Ross, Principal Wilson would like to see you in her office. *Before* the morning bell."

What could I have possibly done wrong now?

The office feels even scarier when the typewriter is quiet and the phone isn't ringing. I knock on Mrs. Wilson's closed door.

"Come in," she says.

I go in. She tells me to sit. I sit.

"This trip we're planning to Clear Creek is an opportunity that comes once every seven years. I'd like all my sixth-graders to benefit from it, Charlie. That includes Armstrong."

Mrs. Wilson looks right at me over the top of her half-round glasses.

"I know you and he have had some conflict this year."

Some? He took Ho Hos out of my lunch. He kicked my ass in front of the school!

"But out of every conflict comes an opportunity."

She continues to look at me over the top of her glasses. "Armstrong will be staying at your house this Friday."

My house? Are you insane? Where? He can't sleep in Lily's room. That's her private space. Andy's room is out of the question. And there's no way he's sharing a room with me.

"I don't know, Mrs. Wilson," I say. "Maybe I should ask my mom."

"Actually," she says, "it was her idea."

Armstrong

Friday afternoon, instead of getting on the long Crown bus, I hop on the short square one with Charlie Ross.

My usual driver is Mr. Simms, who fits the exact description of Leroy Brown in that Jim Croce song. I'd rather meet a junkyard dog any day than mean old Mr. Simms.

The *gentleman* driver of Ross's bus, by contrast, seems like he should be delivering milk to all the white people around here before he drives their kids to school. Got them short sleeves and a Bic pen in the pocket. Glasses so clean you can see right through to his blue eyes.

"Good afternoon, young fellow," he says to me, all friendly and white. "Welcome to my bus."

"Thank you, Mister . . ."

"Orr," he says. "As in either-or, with an extra *r*."

"I'll remember how to spell it," I say. And Ross and I find ourselves a seat halfway back.

You'd expect all the houses in one neighborhood to be more or less the same. But these homes don't really fit together. Each is so different from the next, it's what Mr. Khalil would call a *hodgepodge* of houses. There goes one like a French chateau with a stone lion in front. Across the street is a white cottage with a blue door. Here's one with a red tile roof. Reminds me of Olvera Street, but it's next door to a Brady Bunch house.

I hope the people who live in these houses get along with each other better than the houses seem to.

The bus chugs to the top of a hill. Out the window I see a girl standing on her skateboard, waiting for the bus to pass by. Soon as it does, she rides on.

"We get off here," Ross says.

"Already? Might as well walk. You only got a five-minute ride."

"It isn't safe to walk. There are no sidewalks until halfway up Greenvalley Road."

"You think *this* isn't safe? You should see the walk home from *my* bus stop."

We go on down the street. There's a Mercedes-Benz parked in one driveway, a Corvette in another. Every house got a yard. Every yard got a fence. Most with barking dogs on the other side.

"Say, Ross, which one of these big houses is yours?"

"This one."

We're in front of a black and white two-story house with a steep roof and a chimney so tall I'm worried about hawks crashing. There's a spread of grass and some flowers that look like rolled-up white flags standing on a hill.

The garage has a basketball hoop stuck to it. Now I see where Charlie Ross gets his outside shot.

Only way to describe the inside of his house is a big hug you weren't expecting. The wood panels on the walls and the thick carpet on the floor make you want to kick off your shoes. Armchairs big enough for two and a leather couch that Wilt Chamberlain could stretch out on. The lamps and such are made out of brown wood your hand can't help but stroke as you pass by. And there's other things you'd like to touch but know you shouldn't. Like the miniature painted houses all lined up on a shelf over the fireplace. I'll bet Ross and his brother weren't allowed to even hold a ball in here.

We go into the kitchen, where a brown lady peels carrots at the sink.

"*Hola*, Charlie," she says. "*Que tal?*"

"*Hola*, Lily," Ross says.

Lily looks at me while Ross is searching for the Spanish word to say who I am.

"*Este es mi . . . mi . . .*"

"Amigo?" she says.

"Yeah, *amigo,* I guess. His name's Armstrong."

She gives me an *hola* too.

Now Charlie Ross opens up the cabinet and I see his hand reach for a box of Ho Hos. He glances at me and smiles, and then his hand moves over to the Flaky Flix. Thin chocolate cookies with bumpy rice flakes on the top. I've never tried those, so I'm glad he passed by the Ho Hos.

Ross pours out two glasses of milk and carries everything to the table. I see him dunk his Flaky Flix into the milk, so I try dunking mine too. It's pretty good, but on the next cookie I don't dunk because the milk takes away the crunch, and that's the best part of a Flaky Flix.

There's a yellow poster on the wall, showing a flower and black writing that says WAR IS NOT HEALTHY FOR CHILDREN AND OTHER LIVING THINGS.

"My daddy was in Korea," I say.

"Mine was in World War Two."

"He get hurt?"

"No. He was in the navy, clearing mines in the Pacific, but we dropped the bomb before he saw any action."

"My dad saw some, in Korea."

"Did he get hurt?"

I think about the ways my daddy got hurt by war. A leg blown off. Friends he saw die. The Flashbacks.

War is not healthy for children and other living things. That's the truth.

But what I say to Charlie Ross is, "Yeah, but he can still kick my ass."

He tells me his mom got the poster from her consciousness-raising group.

"What kind of group?"

"Consciousness-raising. It's this group of moms in Laurel Canyon. They get together when the dads play gin. They try to raise their consciousness."

"What's that mean, Ross? How do you raise somebody's consciousness?"

"By making them more aware, I guess."

"What do they talk about?"

"I'm not allowed to listen in."

I just look at him and wait. When a person's got a loose grip on a secret they want to tell, all you have to do is give 'em a small stretch of quiet, and they'll let go.

"Well," Ross says, leaning in to whisper, "there's this one lady whose husband is having an affair, but she won't leave him because she doesn't have money to live on her own. Another one has been drinking too much. They're trying to help her quit."

"And you're not allowed to listen in."

We're about done with the Flaky Flix. I get up and start to clear my plate, but Ross says to just leave it on the table. "Lily will take care of it," he says.

"You know something, Ross," I say. "You need to have *your* consciousness raised."

I carry my own plate to the sink. "Gracias, Armstrong," Lily says.

Charlie

Armstrong asks to see the rest of the house. Maybe I can show him just the downstairs. That way he won't think it's so big. But then, what'll I do tonight when we have to go to sleep? My room is upstairs.

We head into the living room. He stops to look at Mom's painting on the wall. It's of the calla lilies that grow in our backyard. Andy used to cut them for her every Mother's Day. He doesn't just *look* at the painting. He leans forward and sniffs it.

"What are you doing?"

"Stopping to smell the lilies."

"They're not real."

"Look real to me."

He sniffs again. A voice calls to us from a corner of the room.

"Do you like it?"

It's Mom. She's usually still in her bathrobe when I get home. But today she's in powder-blue jeans and an embroidered work shirt. It's a no-bandanna day too, which means she washed her hair.

"I do. But I'm a little worried about it."

"Why?" Mom raises an eyebrow.

"Because I'm allergic to flowers. Those yellow tubes with the pollen on 'em might make me sneeze."

Mom smiles and waves him off. "Oh, go on."

Then I say, "Mom, this is Armstrong. Armstrong, this is my mom."

He steps toward her and puts out his hand. She puts out hers and they shake. Her hand looks small inside his.

"Those your initials in the corner, Mrs. Ross?"

"They are."

"What else do you paint?"

"Not much. Not in a long time, anyway."

"Well, you should start again. If I had a talent like that, I'd paint every day."

Mom looks at Armstrong, and then she shrugs. Like it's a good idea. Like maybe tomorrow. Or another day ahead.

"Are you going to take Armstrong upstairs, Charlie?"

I wish she hadn't said that.

We go up, and Armstrong stops to look at our wall of family pictures. The higher up you look, the further back in time you go—all the way to my great-grandparents on both sides. Near the ceiling is a photo of my great-grandfather sitting on a bench in a Russian village. He has a long white beard and wears a long white robe.

"That your great-granddaddy?"

"Zayde Moishe, they called him."

"Zay-dah who?"

"It's Yiddish. *Zayde* for grandpa. *Moishe* for Moses."

"Damn, he's short. Legs don't even touch the ground. But his beard does."

"He was a rabbi," I say. "Had seven daughters."

"Seven! And look at him now, sitting on the top of the wall."

Armstrong's eyes move slowly down the pictures. "That must be your daddy in a sailor suit." Near the bottom he finds me when I was just five. "And look, they put you in one to match."

He looks back and forth between my young dad and me. "You look a lot like him, Ross."

Then he spots the picture of me and Andy when we were seven and eight. He looks at Andy with his gold-rimmed glasses, long hair, and freckles. He looks at a picture of my mom.

"Your brother, he looks a lot like your mom."

Armstrong's head turns toward the end of the hall, where a sign on a closed door says BEAM ME UP, SCOTTY.

"His bedroom?"

I nod.

"You don't have to show me if you don't want to."

All of a sudden it feels okay to go in. Like I want to, almost. Or Andy wants me to. Not just me, either. Me and Armstrong.

I open the door.

"What's that smell?" Armstrong asks.

"Andy had a darkroom."

I walk over to the closet and pull open the door. The scent of developer and stop bath hits us in our throats. Armstrong leans back, then leans in for a closer look. The enlarger, trays, and supplies are all still there.

"What kind of pictures did he make?"

"Those," I say, pointing back into the room.

We look at the wall over Andy's bed. It's filled with eight-by-tens of seagulls frozen in black and white. When he first got his camera, Andy was crazy for those birds. He'd ask Mom to drive him out to the Santa Monica Pier, where he'd shoot them swooping down on the beach. Later he wondered what it was like to be one, so he started taking pictures from places up high. On countertops. Up on the fire road. In our Thinking Tree.

I'm lost in all these pictures, all these birds, when I hear Armstrong say, "This the camera he used?"

He's found Andy's camera bag and pulled out the Minolta SR-101 that Mom bought him for his eleventh birthday. *That's no kid's camera,* she told him. *A real thirty-five-millimeter single-lens reflex.*

Armstrong looks through the viewfinder at me, then pans around the room. He stops at the wall of pictures. Like he's going to take a picture of a picture.

"Um, Armstrong," I say.

He guesses why. "I wasn't going to shoot one. Just looking through."

He glances at the frame counter on top of the camera. "What's the eleven for?"

"It must still have film in it. The eleven means he shot ten pictures."

"Of what?"

"I don't know."

Armstrong starts to put the camera back into the bag but sees a sheet of paper at the bottom. He unfolds it, and together we look at a ditto from Mrs. Valentine's class.

6th Grade Final Art Project: A Few of Your Favorite Things. Make a collage of your ten favorite things, from drawings you make, photos you take, or images you cut from a magazine. Give each a caption. Arrange them on a poster board. Due date: June 3, 1974.

"You think that's what's on this roll? His favorite things?"

"Could be."

"You should develop it, Ross."

"My mom will when she's ready," I say, putting the handout back into the bag and zipping it shut.

"Listen," Armstrong says, "about that time you told me he died."

"What about it?"

"I wasn't really paying attention. I was just thinking about me."

"That's okay."

"No, it's not. It was wrong. And the thing is, I'm sorry for it."

We look at each other for a minute. It's so quiet we can hear Andy's clock radio click from one minute to the next.

What do you say to someone who never apologizes when they finally do?

"Ever see a naked lady swimming in a pool?"

"Well, you know, Ross, the mind is a powerful place. That's where I *have* seen such a sight. *And* in the occasional magazine."

"How would you like to see one for real?"

"For real real?"

"My across-the-street neighbor is a movie producer. His house has a big wall in back. Behind that wall there's a pool. And every Friday afternoon at four, girls go skinny-dipping there."

Armstrong stares me down like he thinks I'm lying. Then he looks at his watch.

In the 7.1 San Fernando Earthquake four years ago, we got lucky. There was hardly any damage to our house. But there *was* some to our neighbor's wall.

Andy found the crack — and waited a whole year before showing it to me.

"Why didn't you show me sooner?" I asked him.

"You were too young for what's on the other side of that wall."

"And now?"

"Now you're eleven, Charlie. That's old enough."

So, as a kind of birthday present, he showed me what I'm showing Armstrong. We're in the hidden space between the row of cypress trees and the wall. Armstrong's got his eye pressed tight to the hole.

"What are you talking about, naked ladies swimming in the pool? Nothing but empty rafts floating around in there."

"Keep looking."

"Ross, if you dragged me behind these scratchy bushes for a poor man's peep show, and it comes out an empty peep, I am going to kick your ass."

"Keep looking."

"Every Friday at four. Already four-fifteen and the pool's still empty. Kicking your ass won't be enough. I will strip it naked and throw it clear over the top of this wall and into that—"

His mouth stops moving. His eyes go wide. Like everything else about Armstrong Le Rois, his watch is running fast.

"Oh," he says.

"What do you see?"

"Wow!"

"Someone there?"

"That . . . is . . . something."

I hoist myself up and try to nudge him aside. Armstrong shoves me into the branches of the tree.

"Wait your turn, Ross."

He leans a little to the left.

"Oh, my!"

He leans a little to the right.

"Oh double my."

I can hear something skimming through the water, then a splashing that sounds like applause. I try to push in front of Armstrong, but he straight-arms me away.

The applause turns to soft waves against the side of the pool. I hear the *gloop gloop gloop* of water going into the filter.

"Okay, Ross, your turn."

Armstrong leans back. I push him out of the way and peer through the hole.

And what I see is . . . wet footprints leading to the house.

· 11 ·

THE CUSS BOX

Armstrong

BACK AT ROSS MANOR, we're in one of the four bathrooms changing for dinner when Ross informs me that his daddy has *an aversion* to cussing of any kind. "If you use profanity around here," he says, "it'll cost you."

"Cost me what?"

"Depends on the word. Come on, I'll show you."

The dining room table's already set fancy with a white cloth and white plates, silverware, and white napkins. Shiny silver candlesticks hold up brand-new candles. Down at the far end something's hiding under a blue and white cover with strange letters on it. I lift up the fabric and find a big loaf of bread. Looks like a girl's hair in a braid; smells like melted butter.

"The challah's for later," Ross says, like he's bringing up a loogie from the back of his throat.

"The what?"

"Challah," he says again, with that same rasp in his throat. "Egg bread. Only fancy for Friday night."

I tug the cover back over the *ccchallah* while Ross reaches up to this antique hutch they got. He pulls down a wooden box with a slotted rubber plug in the top, like you might see on a piggy bank.

"This is the Cuss Box," he says, holding it close for me to read the poem on the side:

Cussing ain't the nicest thing,
And friends for you it sure don't bring.
But if you really gotta say 'em,
Here's the way you hafta pay 'em:
A mild cuss is just a nickel.
A barroom cuss costs a dime.
For awful cusses you really oughter
Put in the box at least a quarter.

"Don't say I didn't warn you," Ross says.

"You mean you want me to talk white around here."

"Not white. Just clean."

I put the Cuss Box back on the shelf and tell him not to worry. My mama raised me to be polite in front of other people's parents.

But just in case I might slip, I reach down and pat the pocket of my jeans to see do I have a cussing budget.

Charlie

Mom strikes a match and gets ready for the Friday night prayers. I can see Armstrong sitting up straight, like he's witnessing something that's sacred but not his and he doesn't want to get in the way.

But that's not how Mom wants him to feel. "Shabbat is our day of rest, Armstrong," she explains. "We bless the candles, the wine, and the bread to show our appreciation for light, laughter, and food."

She lights the candles and then covers her eyes while saying a prayer.

"Baruch atah Adonai, eloheinu melech ha'olam, asher kidishanu b'mitz votav, vitzivanu, l'chad lich nehr, shel Shabbat."

She pours grape juice for Armstrong and me and wine for herself but not for my dad. To him alcohol is like live electricity, a thing never to be touched. "It impairs your judgment, Charlie," he always says.

"Baruch atah Adonai, eloheinu melech ha'olam, boray p'ree hagofin."

She sips her wine, we sip our juice. She puts her hand on the embroidered cloth that my grandma made in 1900. The Hebrew letters spell out "challah."

"Baruch atah Adonai, eloheinu melech ha'olam, hamostzi l'chem min ha'aretz. Amen."

She lifts the cover like she's revealing a prize. Armstrong says "Amen" too.

Mom breaks off a piece of bread, and from this piece she breaks off a small piece for herself before passing the rest around the table. When we've all taken some for ourselves, we eat.

"Can we get a second piece of *ccchallah?*" Armstrong whispers to me. I say sure and reach for some more, accidentally knocking over my grape juice.

"Dammit!" I say, sliding back from the table and stopping most of the spill with my napkin.

"Charlie." Dad nods toward the Cuss Box.

I get up, go over, and drop in a nickel. I look at Armstrong as if to say, *See?*

Armstrong nods, and I sit back down.

"Well, boys, what stood out for you about this day?" my father asks like he always does. Only this time it's "boys" again instead of just "Charlie."

"We found out something in Andy's room," I say. "Actually, Armstrong found it out."

Mom and Dad look at Armstrong.

"It's about his camera, Mrs. Ross. It was there in the case by his bed, and I was curious because I've never held a camera like that before."

Mom takes a sip of wine.

"There's still film in it. The window on top shows he shot ten pictures. Tell what else we found, Ross."

"A handout in his bag," I say. "From Mrs. Valentine's class last year. A Favorite Things project. That's probably what's on his roll."

"Are you going to develop them, Mrs. Ross?" Armstrong asks.

"Someday," Mom says with her rubber-band smile.

Dad asks what else we did today, and Armstrong glances at me, one eyebrow up, and grins. "Well, Mr. Ross, the highlight for me was the *promenade* we took through your neighborhood. A lot of lovely things to see."

Under the table, I drive the toe of my tennis shoe as hard as I can into Armstrong's leg. He grins through the pain.

"What did Charlie show you?" Mom asks.

"Well, Mrs. Ross, there are some nice houses on this street. And the view in some of the back yards, now that's something I don't get to see much of at home. Why, for instance, did you know that just across the street here—"

"Have some more *chicken*, Armstrong," I say, dropping a drumstick onto his plate.

"Thank you, Charles. What I was saying is, across the street is a long driveway, and up that driveway you can see—"

"You're out of mashed potatoes, too." I ladle some more next to his drumstick.

"What did you see?" Dad asks.

"Why don't we let Armstrong eat his dinner before it gets cold?"

"I might be hungry for the food," Armstrong says, "but your mom and dad are hungry for the story. You tell it, Ross, while I eat."

Armstrong

This is going to be fun. Eating mashed potatoes and *ccchallah* while Ross tells what he showed me across the street. I know he won't want to lie on the Sabbath. Won't want to tell the truth either. I wonder which one he'll get caught in.

"I took Armstrong across the street," he says, "and we looked into Reggie's back yard."

"That's snooping, Charlie," Mr. Ross says. "You shouldn't have done that."

"What did you see?" Mrs. Ross asks. She's curious like her son.

"A swimming pool," Ross says. "An *empty* swimming pool."

"What did *you* see, Armstrong?"

"I saw one of the Lord's most attractive creations."

"Yeah?"

"Something every boy ought to see at least once."

"Which is . . . ?"

"Sunlight on clean blue water."

"That's *all* you saw?" Ross says, all surprised.

"That and the pool man cleaning the pool. You must've got the day of the week wrong, Ross."

Charlie

The best part of Shabbat dinner is the dessert. That's when my father serves some fabulous sweet he's either baked or brought home from Viktor Benês Bakery near his store.

I ask him if he stopped at the bakery. Maybe he picked up some black and white cookies or chocolate-chip rolls.

"The line was too long. There's a box of Flaky Flix in the pantry, though."

Armstrong and I look at each other. Half a box, maybe.

"And you're welcome to eat a common store-bought cookie if you like. Or you can have a slice of the Neverfail."

My father baked!

He gets up from the table and goes into the kitchen. Soon he's back carrying the glass cake stand that my parents got for their wedding. He sets the Neverfail in front of Armstrong.

"I've always let the boys slice their own," my dad says, handing Armstrong a silver spatula. "You can slice your own too, Armstrong. But you're on the honor system."

The *honor system* is a policy our dad came up with when, many cakes ago, Andy and I got into a fight over whose slice was bigger. I said his was; he said mine was. We started stealing bites off each other's plates. When the plates were empty, we went on fighting for a bigger piece. Like savage animals going for the last scrap, we bit and clawed each other until I, smaller but faster, squirmed free and dived for the cake, landing mouth first but knocking over the stand. The Neverfail was in ruins.

The next cake was served on the honor system. Instead of handing us our own slices, Dad handed us knives! He told us to "cut your own slices. But remember, boys, you're on the honor system."

We translated *honor system* to mean *as-much-as-you-want system*. We cut such big slices that there was nothing left on the stand but crumbs. Thirty minutes later we took turns barfing into the toilet.

Months went by, and at Thanksgiving the honor system was again announced. This time we made smaller cuts. From cake to cake, our self-guided slices grew thinner, more honorable.

Armstrong holds the silver spatula, eyeing the great round cake before him.

"You mean I can cut my own?" he says.

"That's right. On the honor system."

Armstrong

I'm wondering, is it honorable to use the knife as a fork and call the whole damn cake my slice? But the *whole* cake for me would be greedy, and Papa Ross and the Mrs. are waiting their turn. So I line up that knife about halfway across the cake. I figure since it's my first time I should get half and the three of them can divide the rest. But then I start thinking about Lily in the kitchen, waiting *her* turn. So I move the knife back a bit, making my piece about one-third the size of the cake.

It still feels like a selfish slice. And what if Papa Ross's Neverfail *looks* good but tastes like dust? Then I'll be stuck having to eat it all just to be polite. I move the knife over to the left. But that looks like the kind of slice Otis would take, all twiggy, like his legs. Back over to the right some. That looks like a good, hungry boy's slice of cake. But what if this cake really is as good as Ross said? Then I'm going to be wanting more, but if we start out on the honor system and then ask for seconds, is that dishonorable? Little more to the right. That's good. Small enough to satisfy Mr. Khalil if he was watching. Big enough to satisfy me.

That's where I start to saw. But you don't need to *saw* one of Papa Ross's cakes. It's so light and moist, gravity makes the cut for you. My hand is just the guide. Pretty soon I'm lifting my *honorably* sliced piece onto my plate.

The whole Ross family is staring at me like I'm on TV.

Charlie

Armstrong's fork breaks off a square and lifts some cake to his mouth. We watch the cake float past his lips. We watch the bite go in.

He doesn't say a word. You can see tiny bulges appear and disappear inside his cheeks, his lips, and just above his chin as his tongue roams around the inside of his mouth. He looks at his plate, then takes a second bite. This time, as the fork comes out it gets stopped by his teeth, which bite down on the tines, scraping them clean.

Still no verdict. Here comes a third bite. Armstrong's eyes never leave his plate. Our eyes never leave him. Soon there's nothing left but crumbs and a streak of frosting. He presses the back of the fork onto the crumbs, drags them to the edge of the plate, and brings them up to his mouth for his final bite.

"Well?" my father asks. "What do you think?"

Armstrong sets down his fork slowly, like a kid giving up a toy at the end of a turn. Then he drinks the whole glass of milk my mom poured for him, cleans the corners of his mouth with his napkin, and looks straight at my dad.

"Mr. Ross," he says, reaching into the pocket of his jeans, "that was the finest . . . "

He looks at the shiny coin in his hand.

"The most— . . . "

He rubs the coin between his finger and his thumb. He takes a deep breath, sighs, and shakes his head.

"It was the BEST GODDAMN CAKE I'VE EVER HAD!"

He drops a quarter into the Cuss Box and we all bust up, as Armstrong would say, laughing, really laughing, all of us, for the first time in a long time.

Armstrong

After dinner we go up to Charlie Ross's bedroom. I see some Hardy Boys books, a record player with some speakers attached to it, and a Nerf hoop hanging from the closet door. On the wall beside his bed he's got a signed poster of Roman Gabriel, which is nice but would be nicer if it was Deacon Jones.

"You don't got a TV in your room?" I say.

"Do you in yours?"

"Oh, yes. Sometimes I let my sisters watch it. And sometimes I let my mama and daddy, too."

"That's lucky. I have to watch in my parents' room or downstairs with my dad."

Ross finishes packing his bag for Clear Creek. Toothbrush and toothpaste go in one plastic baggie, hairbrush in another. That's something I never have to give much thought to: my hair. But Ross has so much of it, long and wavy, he probably loses time every morning getting it right. Whenever we play basketball, he has to dribble with one hand and whisk the hair out of his eyes with the other. That's how I know he's about to shoot. If he got a haircut, he'd be harder to guard.

He opens up a drawer in his desk, takes out some batteries and a pair of walkie-talkies, changes the batteries, and tosses the walkies into his bag. Then he zips up the duffle and sets it on the floor next to mine.

Now, his bedroom has got two beds. One is a single bed like my sisters get to sleep in at home. Long enough for growing legs, high enough to keep the dust out of your nose. It's made up with the pillows tucked under the bedspread and a squeaky stuffed dog peeking out from underneath.

Next to that is an army cot. Looks like a half-thick mattress on chicken wire with wheels under the metal frame. Nothing on it but a blanket and a pillow and already it's starting to sag.

"You expecting a soldier?" I ask.

"What do you mean?"

"What exactly is that thing?"

"A rollaway bed."

"Where does it roll away to?"

"A closet, when it's not being used. My dad rents them to his customers when they've got around-the-clock nursing. That way the night nurse has someplace to stretch out."

"I see," I say. "Which one of us is going to be the nurse?"

Charlie Ross blinks a few times like he doesn't comprehend the question.

"I mean, which one of us will be attempting to sleep on that thing?"

"I don't sleep well on a rollaway," he says.

"Who does? But the thing is, Ross, *etiquette*."

"Etiquette?"

"Etiquette says you give the guest the good bed. But since you're already showing me a lot of hospitality—for which I'm grateful—toss me that Nerf ball. We'll start the game at sixteen–nothing, you in the lead. First one to twenty gets the good bed."

"There's no room for a court."

"We're playing rugby hoops. It's a game I just made up. You take it out over there by your desk. You can be traveling, jumping up onto the beds, rolling across the floor—any method of transportation you want. All you got to do is get the ball in the hoop. I'll even let you take it out."

I toss him the ball.

He steps back to his desk, then leaps onto his bed, and that's when I ram my shoulder into his thigh like Deacon Jones would do, flipping him onto his back. Then I Indian-burn his wrist. He lets go of the Nerf, and I fly up to the hoop. Slam dunk.

We're five minutes late to bed. It takes me that long to

score the rest of the points and tuck Ross into the rollaway, along with his little stuffed dog to comfort him after his loss.

The door opens and Mrs. Ross steps in, wearing Andy's camera around her neck. She holds up a powder-blue jacket, all puffy like it's full of feathers.

"This was Andy's parka," she says. "Your Windbreaker will be warm enough during the day, Armstrong. But I checked the weather and the nights might get cold. Would you like to take this along?"

"You sure you want to let it out of the house?"

"I'm sure."

"I appreciate that, Mrs. Ross. I'll take good care of it."

She sets the jacket on my duffle bag and says, "Good night, Armstrong. Good night, Charlie."

She says it in one breath, like we're brothers.

After a few minutes of lying beside him in the dark, I say, "Ross?"

"Yeah?"

"Thank you."

"For what, missing almost every shot I took?"

"For volunteering to have me stay at your house."

Charlie

I'm awake half the night, wishing that I did.

· 12 ·

CLEAR CREEK

Armstrong

EARLY SATURDAY MORNING WE STEP onto the long bus and make our way down the aisle. Ross and I call the back bench. Otis and Alex are the only ones we'll share with. Otis because he's got work to do — he promised everybody he'd finish up their astrology charts on the ride to Clear Creek — and Alex because we want to know what kind of snacks he brought.

Now, Leslie is sitting halfway up the bus. Got her left arm resting on the seatback, dark hair spilling over it like smoke. And Charlie Ross is *mesmerized*. Probably wishing he could move up there and sniff her.

"You're stuck on the wrong girl," I tell him. "If you want to *learn* something, aim your eyes on the left side of the bus, up there toward the front."

Ross's head turns to look. Eyes double in size.

"Mrs. Gaines!?"

"Not the Yard Supervisor. The girl by her side."

"Shelley?"

"Uh-huh."

"Shelley with the green hair?"

"That's right."

"And freckles on her face?"

"Yep."

"You're crazy."

"She ain't *that* ugly, Ross. She's starting to develop."

"Oh, please."

Then Ross starts in about how in kindergarten they called her Four Eyes. In first grade she was Freckle Face. In second grade she was Four-Eyed Freckle Face. By the third grade they called her Shelley Smelly Belly Button. She was Silly String Hair in fourth, Fish Eyes in fifth, and Class Clown in sixth—on account of the pimple she brought to school one day, on the tip of her nose.

"I see," I say, "so you thought up a bunch of cruel names for her. Did you know she's the smartest person in the school?"

"She is not."

"Is too. That's how come she covers up her tests when they come back. Hundred percent on every one."

"Why hide it, then?"

"'Cause she's classy, that's why."

"Well, I don't like it when she chases me. She'll kiss me if I get caught."

"What's wrong with that?"

"She keeps a pencil tucked behind her ear."

"Ross, you don't know what you've been missing."

"How would you know what I've been missing?"

"I know what I know."

"Which is?"

"She likes two kinds of Now and Laters: watermelon and lime. If a cherry or grape comes up in the pack, she'll offer it to you. She's got green hair—you're right about that—but it's only green from the chlorine in her swimming pool. She washes it every day with Hawaiian Tropic shampoo. And I know she's got those twig lips you think aren't worth a smack, but when they pucker up, they come with a surprise."

"What kind of surprise?"

"Gonna have to let her catch you to find out."

Just for the record, I made that last part up. I've never kissed Shelley.

Charlie

On the freeway toward Glendale and Pasadena, Armstrong points out the window. "That's the San Gabriel Mountains," he says. "I looked it up in Mr. Khalil's atlas. The camp where we're headed has an elevation of two thousand three hundred seventy-four feet. Not much chance of snow this time of year, but the weatherman's talking about rain on Wednesday."

I tell him how, from the Club, most days are too smoggy to see the San Gabriels. He says that from his house you couldn't see them even if it was clear.

"Downtown standing in the way."

"Is this your first time away from home?" I ask.

"I'm away from home every day I come to your school."

At Glendale the bus sails onto Highway 2, northbound. "Getting colder out," Armstrong reports, touching his hand to the glass. A trucker misreads the gesture and gives him a friendly honk.

Up the long aisle I can see through the driver's window. The road ahead is empty, except for the round back of another Crown bus, the same yellow-orange as ours. Mrs. Wilson said that Wonderland wasn't the only school that would be spending a week at Clear Creek. One other school was chosen too.

I start to wonder about the other kids who'll be there. What if the second school is Holmes Avenue, Armstrong's neighborhood school? Will he feel like he belongs with them, or with us?

I stretch my neck for a better look at the other bus, but we're too far behind to see any faces inside.

Then Otis slides into the seat in front of me. "Done with your chart," he says.

He unfolds a piece of wrinkled paper that you can tell

he's spent a lot of time on. At the top, in his large block letters, is my name and birth date. Underneath is a long paragraph in neat handwriting, all about me.

Charlie Ross, you are a Cancer. Cancers are
homebodies, which means you are happiest when you
are at home. Cancers are sensitive, which means
you care about other people. You care about them
sometimes even more than you care about yourself.
Your zodiac animal is the crab and that shows how
you move through life: side to side. It means you
don't like to stand up to people. You go with the
flow. But sometimes the flow can lead you the
wrong way. So be careful picking your friends. Your
birthday comes just after the middle of the month,
which means you got some qualities of Leo in you
too. Deep down, so far you can't always see it,
there's a lot of courage in you. That comes from
the lion inside. But most times, you want everybody
to like you, so your lion stays in its den. Since
you're sensitive, you're real popular with the girls.
But stay away from the Taurus ones 'cause they
get emotional, which you, being sensitive, take to
heart. What you need in a girlfriend is a Sagittarius
because they are easygoing and just a little dangerous
—not afraid of taking a risk or bending the rules.

I, Otis Greene, your astrological advisor, think

you are a good friend, to me and to Armstrong. You made us feel welcome at our new school.

It's probably the nicest letter I've ever gotten. But one thing about it bothers me.

"Is it true I'm afraid to stand up to people?"

"Your astrology is the tendencies you've got, Charlie. Some people tend toward 'em. Some tend away. It's mostly up to you."

Armstrong has been reading so far over my shoulder, I feel like I've got an extra head. Now he slides out of his seat, drifts up the aisle, and sits behind Shelley.

In a voice he's sure I'll hear, he says, "SAY, SHELLEY, WHAT SIGN OF ASTROLOGY ARE YOU?"

Shelley turns around, blinks twice, and pushes her glasses back up her nose.

"Sagittarius," she says.

Armstrong looks down the aisle at me. He doesn't leave any of his teeth out of the biggest *I told you so* grin he can give.

Armstrong

After he gives Charlie Ross his astrology report, Otis goes up and down the aisle, handing out charts to everybody but me. The bus gets real quiet. Paper airplanes crash. Space Food

Sticks go back into bags. No more singing about bottles of beer on the wall. All heads are bowed to study the charts Otis made.

I don't know much about astrology. But from what I see, it's got the power to put people together. Soon heads are up again, looking around the bus. Hands reaching out to tap shoulders. Same question going around, just in different ways.

"Hey, Melanie, what sign are you?"

"Hey, Christopher, what's your sign?"

"When's your birthday, Jason?"

Ever since Charlie Ross heard he goes well with Sagittarius, and ever since Shelley said that was her sign, he's been looking at her with a new set of eyes. Not the loving kind—yet—but the wondering kind. Like his curiosity got stirred by what Otis said. Now here we are, waiting to get off the bus, and he's right behind her in the aisle. How'd he get up there so fast? Floated on Otis's words, that's how. Just one hint that two people might be a good match makes them pay a different kind of attention. Who knows if it'll go beyond the floating phase? It might just crash like those paper planes. But look at that—his arm is brushing up against hers. Would that have happened without astrology?

I told Otis I don't want to know which sign is right for me. I'd rather find out on my own. For instance, we're not the only school here. A whole other sixth grade just got off a whole other bus. I don't know about the birthdays or the personalities or the general fineness of the girls on that bus, but I am looking to find out. Maybe I'll say hello to one, see where it goes.

We come off our bus and see a crowd of other kids with their bags packed, waiting to get on. Looks like their week in the mountains is done.

"How was it?" I hear Alex Levinson call out.

"Awesome!"

"Bitchin'!"

"You get to watch an owl eat a live rat."

The trees stand taller up here than in the Canyon where Ross lives. They're pines, and you can hear the wind telling secrets through their branches. Way up past the top of one, I see blue sky.

Soon as we get our bags from under the bus, Mr. Mitchell leads the boys' line and Mrs. Valentine and Mrs. Gaines lead the girls'.

"The cabins are across the river," a guide tells us, "a quarter mile from here. There are five girls' cabins and five boys'. You'll be mixed in with kids from the other school, a chance to make new friends."

We cross a bridge and go along the banks of the stream, past trees and more trees. Sound of water running over rocks means one thing: beauty rest tonight.

Mrs. Valentine and Mrs. Gaines take the girls into their cabins. Mr. Mitchell takes us into ours. Me and Ross land in the same one. Otis, too.

The boys from the other school are already flipping coins for top or bottom bunk. Digging sweaters from their duffles. Got their backs to us when we come in. But all at once they turn around, and all at once I see this is not one of the schools that had Opportunity Busing.

Every last face is white.

And then a surprising thing happens. Charlie Ross steps up to one of the boys and says, "Keith?"

"Charlie Ross! What are you doing here?"

They do a little high-five, and then Ross says, "Wonderland got picked for Clear Creek this week."

"Carpenter too." Then the boy who goes by Keith turns to his friends already kicked back on bottom bunks. "Tim, Randy, you remember Charlie Ross."

They slouch over and say hello.

Then Keith's eyes slide over to Otis and me.

"Which one of you is Armstrong?"

"That's me," I say.

"Charlie Ross told me all about you."

Ross's cheeks catch fire, like maybe he didn't say the nicest things about me.

Out comes Keith's hand with an open palm, and we shake. It ain't no soft shake neither, I can tell you that.

· 13 ·

SPIN-THE-BOTTLE

Charlie

"Erosion is happening all the time," Cody, one of the naturalists, tells us. We're standing by the bank of a stream, and he has to shout over the rushing water. "Does anybody know the three types of rocks?"

In Mr. Mitchell's classroom, Armstrong's arm usually rests on the table or in his lap, too heavy to lift. But here it floats right up. Cody calls on him.

"Well," Armstrong says, "first you got the kind a volcano spits up. They start out as lava, but when that cools, rocks start to form and these they call *igneous*. The shiny kind. Then there's ones come from layers of sand resting on each other and over time getting packed down tight. Toss 'em against the wall and they crumble. That's the *sedimentary*. And these here"—he bends down and picks up a rock, turning it over in his fingers—"the river makes. They're called *metamorphic*, and they make good skipping stones when the river's calm."

Armstrong flings a rock toward the river. The rock gets swallowed up by the fast-moving stream.

"Well, guys," Cody says, "I think I can take the morning off. You already got yourself a guide."

Armstrong smiles. I notice one of the Carpenter girls in the back looking at him. She's got blond hair and topaz eyes. The hair cut short for spring. It's Jodie St. Claire.

"Hands off, Charlie Ross."

Keith hovers right behind me, looking in the same direction. He tells me he asked Jodie to go steady and she said yes.

Cody loops his arm through the air, motioning for us to follow. We make our way up a winding trail to the highest point at Clear Creek: the camp's observatory and weather station. The observatory is a converted water tank, with a fat telescope aimed at the sky.

"We'll be back here tonight," Cody says, "to have a closer look at the stars."

Otis nudges Alex with excitement. He can't wait to see the stars up close.

"Might not see much, Cody," a voice calls from across the room.

Armstrong is standing in front of three round gauges —barometer, wind speed, temperature—giving the forecast. "Pressure's dropping. We could get a storm tonight."

I feel a tap on my shoulder. In his old playful way Keith springs toward me, and I jump back.

"Two for flinching." He grins and slugs me twice on the

shoulder. He nods toward Armstrong. "You never told me the new kid's so uppity," he says.

Uppity. It sounds like a word to put someone down.

"He's all right. Actually he's—"

"A know-it-all is what he is. You should've kicked his ass the first week of school. If he gives you any trouble up here, me and Randy and Tim'll take care of him."

Keith smiles like he's looking forward to a bad thing.

Armstrong was right about the forecast. By dinnertime it starts to rain, and the stargazing gets postponed. Instead we're going to watch a movie about coyotes, hawks, and other predators of Southern California. As we go through the cafeteria line, word spreads that some of the Wonderland girls have scoped out a toolshed near their cabins. The invitation is on for spin-the-bottle.

During the movie, I slide down low in my chair and crawl out the back door. I walk the path to the shed, taking in icy breaths of air and puffing out steam. It's around seven at night. I shut my eyes and picture the streetlight in front of my house turning on. Then I push open the door to the shed.

Leslie Maduros is there, holding a flashlight in her lap. So are Denise Wynn, Melanie Bates, Susan Campbell, and Jason Vale. I think Jason's a little disappointed when he sees me walk in, since he was the only boy.

The rain is drumming on the tin roof and there's no heat in the shed, so we make the circle tighter and the mood is just right . . . except we have nothing to spin. We look around for a substitute bottle. The rakes, shovels, axes, and hoes are too heavy, too big.

"We could play spin-the-shoe," I say. But my idea is a dud.

The door opens. Leslie shines her flashlight on a pair of lopsided glasses.

"What are you guys doing?" Shelley says, sipping chocolate milk from a carton.

"Playing spin-the-bottle," I say. "Except we don't have one to spin."

"Can I play?"

I scoot over to make room for her.

"Sorry," Denise says, "we've got enough girls."

Shelley shrugs like she's used to being kept out of a circle. She sits by herself on the other side of the shed.

"We could get a rock or a twig from outside," Leslie suggests.

"A rock won't spin straight," Jason says. "And a twig's too easy to control."

Across the shed, I notice Shelley leaning all the way back to get the last sip of chocolate milk. I never knew her skin was so white.

The door opens again. Alex Levinson fills the frame.

"A Space Food Stick!" I say. "Alex, got one on you?"

"I ate the last one this morning."

There's a loud pop, like a balloon getting stuck by a pin.

We all turn to see Shelley bending over and picking up the flattened milk carton she just stomped on.

"Hey, guys. Whatcha doing?" Janelle Parson drifts in.

"Playing spin-the-bottle."

"Can I play?"

"Got anything to spin?"

"Why not use your flashlight?"

Leslie sets the flashlight on the floor and gives it a spin. Its beam whips around like a strobe light.

When it stops, one face swims out of the darkness: Jason Vale's. As Leslie scoots toward him, her knee bumps the flashlight, and suddenly it's real quiet in the shed. I don't know what's worse, the kiss I can't see or the one I can in my mind.

Meanwhile, Shelley is pulling the pencil from behind her ear and twisting the point against the flattened milk carton. Soon a hole opens and the pencil pops through.

"Your turn, Charlie," Jason says. I shine the light at him, his lips still moist from Leslie's kiss. I feel a little sick inside and hope the light goes past Leslie to land on some other girl.

The beam whirls around and around and around once more before it lands on Alex Levinson. A boy-to-boy spin is an automatic do-over. On my next try the beam stops between Jason and Alex. I follow the light to the far end of the shed, where I can see Shelley sitting by herself, drawing an arrow on one side of her milk carton. She pushes the pencil tip back through the hole and twists it between planks in the floor. Then she loads her middle finger under her thumb and flicks a corner of the carton. The waxy cardboard twirls around and around, a perfect homemade spinner.

Her spinner stops and Shelley looks up. The arrow is pointing at me.

Armstrong

That's one thing I forgot to pack: a flashlight. But Otis brought one, and soon as the movie's done we head outside for a walk. See a low light coming from a shed over by the girls' cabins.

"What you think they got going on in there?" Otis says.

"Only one way to find out."

When we pull open the door, it's obvious what they got going on in there: spin-the-flashlight.

"Got room in that circle for two more?" I say.

There's a little pause. "Sorry," Leslie says. "Circle's full."

I *told* Ross he's stuck on the wrong girl. But now the right one says, "There's room in mine."

Otis and I sit beside Shelley. Looks like she made herself a spinner out of a milk carton. Girl might not be so handy with a handball, but she's handy with her head.

"Still your spin, Charlie," Leslie says over at the other circle. She drags a ChapStick across her lips and gives Ross a glossy smile.

The door opens. A couple of Carpenter girls come in,

both of 'em fine. One is a blond girl I noticed before. The other's got a little flap of bangs on her forehead like something you might want to peek under.

"Spin-the-bottle," the blond girl says. "Cool."

They sit over by Shelley.

From the other circle I hear somebody say, "Charlie, aren't you going to spin?"

Ross seems to think about that. Then he says, "They're short a boy in that circle."

And he slides over to ours.

Charlie

Otis spins first. Shelley's carton whirls around and around. When it stops, the arrow is pointing at Jodie's friend, the girl with the bangs.

She smiles at Otis and says, "I'm Nancy."

"I'm Otis. What sign are you, Nancy?"

"Pisces."

"Libra. This oughta be a good kiss."

He puts a hand on her arm and pulls her gently toward him. They kiss like it's not their first time.

"Your turn, Charlie."

Shelley points at the spinner she made. I close my eyes and get a nervous feeling. I spin. The carton whirls around. I open my eyes.

It's Shelley. She takes hold of my sweatshirt and tugs me toward her. Our mouths collide. Our teeth clink.

"I'm sorry," she whispers, and then it's just our lips touching.

The funny part is, they're kind of soft. And warm. And moist in a good, not gross, way. Her breath smells sweet — watermelon and lime Now and Laters aren't her only flavor. She likes banana, too.

She runs her fingers through my hair. I get a warm feeling down my neck.

"We playing spin-the-bottle here, or seven minutes in heaven?" Armstrong butts in.

Shelley's lips pull away from mine, but our eyes keep looking at each other. Even though it's dark here in the shed, I suddenly remember that her eyes are peppermint green.

Peppermint green is my new favorite color.

Armstrong spins next and lands on Otis. "You know I love you, Otis," Armstrong says, "but you had a sloppy joe for lunch, and I ain't kissing that."

He spins again and lands on me. "I love you too, Ross. But it's more of a brotherly love than a lip-to-lip thing."

The next spin lands on himself. He smiles, brings his arm to his lips, and starts kiss-kiss-kissing himself with loud smacks and a soft moan.

The girls in our circle all laugh.

Then Jodie St. Claire moves the milk carton a quarter turn so the arrow is pointing at her.

From across the shed, Leslie shines her flashlight on Armstrong and Jodie. Their lips come together and apart, together again and apart, like they're tasting something neither one has ever tried. They must like it, because soon their heads are moving in a slow orbit all their own. Down below, in Jodie's lap, their hands form a black and white braid.

From somewhere outside, a transistor radio plays "Delta Dawn".

Music and wind suddenly blast through the open door. The music snaps off, but the wind keeps blowing.

Keith stands in the doorway, watching the end of the kiss.

"I've been looking for you, Jodie," he says.

"Well, you found me."

Keith looks at her. He looks at Armstrong. He looks at me.

"I sure did," he says, and backs out into the rain.

Armstrong

I didn't know she had a boyfriend. I especially didn't know it would be *him*.

· 14 ·

A LION COMES OUT

Charlie

"I FELT LIKE THROWING UP."

"You'd throw up even if a white guy kissed her."

"No. I might be jealous. But what I feel now is gross."

We're in the boys' bathroom for shower hour. I step out of a cloud of steam and reach for my towel.

"What do you think, Charlie Ross?" Keith says. "Wasn't it disgusting for Armstrong and Jodie to kiss?"

It's a cheap camp towel, too small to wrap all the way around me. I try to tuck in the corner, but it comes undone.

"Charlie?"

"Huh?"

"I said, don't you think it's gross for them to kiss?"

Randy, Tim, and Keith wait for my answer. I think back to the shed. To the way Armstrong and Jodie kissed. Like they were older than the rest of us, and in their own private world.

"I guess I would be upset," I say, "if somebody else kissed my girl."

Maybe if I were wearing a decent-size towel, I could have said more.

Armstrong

Soon as the lights go out in our cabin, I toss one of the walkie-talkies up to the top bunk.

"Say, Ross," I say into mine, "I know you're glad you joined our circle. Over."

"I had an okay time," he says into his. "Over."

"There must be something wrong with the reception down here. Over?"

"Okay, so maybe I'm a little in love. Over."

"With that pasty-skinned, four-eyed, freckle-faced, stumble-toed, pencil-behind-the-ear Shelley Smelly Belly Button? Over."

"Yeah, with Shelley. Over."

"I told you she was fine. Over."

"What about you and Jodie? Over."

"She's fine too. No doubt about that. And she kisses real sweet. But I know my first taste was my last. Over."

"Why? Over."

"Figure it out, Ross. Over."

"'Cause she's taken? Over."

"That's part of it. Over."

I stare at the wood slats over my head, the ones holding up Charlie Ross's bunk.

"I suppose Surfer Boy'll try to kick my ass," I say. "Over."

I wait for Ross to answer. Wait some more.

"Good thing I got you to back me up," I say. "Over and out."

Charlie

The sun breaks through the next day, but we don't get to see the owl swallow a live rat. It's probably still digesting its last meal and won't eat again till after we're gone.

There isn't any fight between Keith and Armstrong, either. The only fight we see is one between Keith and Jodie, and the only punch thrown is hers — straight from a paper cup into his face. Their relationship ends in a splash.

The one between Armstrong and Jodie ends just as fast. They've been sitting at separate tables in the cafeteria, at opposite sides of Cody's science circle, and in far-apart saddles on the daily horseback ride at dusk to Pine Hill. Whatever else they might have been pretty much ended the minute Keith walked into that shed.

I've been luckier. At breakfast I eat my Quisp cereal with one hand. The other is under the table, holding Shelley's.

I'm not a very good listener during Cody's talks on the food chain, water cycle, climate zones, or mating habits of reptiles. I'm into a mating habit of my own, with my left knee pressed against Shelley's right one. I hope Mr. Mitchell isn't planning to test us on this stuff.

During the rest of the week, we cycle through the camp's "wheel of wonder," which consists of five different science activities: botany bingo; animal improv; nature walk with a naturalist; microscope mysteries; and blind scientist, in which you have to guess the animal by touch alone.

When it's my turn to wear the blindfold, they hand me something slippery and cool and too thick for my fingers to reach all the way around. I feel it moving through my soft grip, winding up my arm and along the back of my neck. My whole body goes numb with fear. "It's a s-s-snake," I stammer.

Afterward, to calm myself down, I go into the aviary and hold a dove.

After that, I hold Shelley's hand.

Thursday morning we all take a walk to the archery range. The counselors put us into ten teams, Wonderland kids and Carpenter kids all mixed together. I wind up on a team with Keith and Randy; Armstrong lands on one with Jodie, Shelley, Denise, and three other Carpenter girls. Win or lose, he's happy as the only boy.

It comes down to our team against Armstrong's. Guess who fires the winning shot.

Not me.

Not Keith.

Not Armstrong.

Not Otis.

It's Shelley! She's what Cody calls a "knacktural." Has a knack for finding the dead center of a circle.

That night, our last one at Clear Creek, Armstrong and I hike up to Pine Hill alone. We lean against a fallen tree trunk, our hands pillowing our heads, and look up at the sky. Instead of clouds, it's all stars.

One streaks overhead. "Shooting star!" Armstrong says. "Old Mr. Khalil told me a legend about shooting stars. Every time you see one, that's a new soul coming to be born."

"There's no proof of that."

"Damn, Ross, why spoil the idea? It's a legend, is all."

"Sorry," I say. "It's hard to believe in stuff like that after you've lost someone."

It's cold out and we shift a little closer to each other. I can feel the sleeve of Andy's parka through my own.

"Okay if I ask how it happened?"

I've never really talked about how Andy died. People asked me if I wanted to, but it was always grownups, never kids. So I always said no.

"Number seven," I say.

"Seven?"

"Of the leading causes of death for kids aged ten to fourteen. Number one is unintentional injuries. He died of number seven: chronic low respiratory disease."

"What is that?"

"Asthma. Andy had bad allergies all his life. It's why he never went to summer camp. Why we couldn't have a dog. Or carpeting in his room. What's weird is that the one place he could breathe easy was his darkroom. Everywhere else he suffered. He took shots and pills, but the pills made him tired all the time.

"My dad brought home a vaporizer from Ross Rents. Andy would fall asleep with it puffing cool mist into the air. My job was to keep water above the line until his breathing eased. My other job was to tell him stories. *Stories about us,* he'd say.

"So I'd tell him about the time the house across the street caught fire twice in the same night. Or about the neighbors who came home drunk and stole our plants. Or the naked lady who knocked on the door. I'd tell him about the night the car broke down on the way to Mammoth and our dad had to walk two miles in a blizzard to bring back help. Mom, Andy, and I sat in the car telling silly knock-knock jokes. The laughter kept us warm.

"The stories, Andy said, helped him breathe.

"Around a year ago, the doctor wanted to try a new medicine. An inhaler instead of pills. For the first few months it worked great. Andy was the old Andy. Taking pictures from trees. Spending time with his girlfriend at their fort. But then he started getting asthma attacks. They got so bad he'd have to spend a night in the hospital.

"On the last Friday of May, he was playing handball on the lower yard, and he just collapsed. Mrs. Wilson called the paramedics. They took him to the hospital, but in the middle of the night he stopped breathing. He didn't come home."

"That's a terrible thing, Ross," Armstrong says. "A terrible, unfair thing."

"Every day I wonder, where did he go? How can someone just be gone?"

We lie there, looking at the sky. It's silent up there. Silent down here, too.

Then Armstrong says, "I almost had a brother."

I turn my head to look at him.

"It's one of my early memories. Putting my hand on Mama's swollen-up belly. I even felt him kick. *Your brother's going to be a kickboxer,* Mama said."

"What happened?"

"He was born still. The cord, they said, got wrapped around his neck."

We keep looking up. But we don't see any more shooting stars.

"Should we go back?" Armstrong says.

"Give it a minute," I say.

Two more go by. Maybe three. And then I see it—a silent streak of light. There for a second, then gone.

I nudge Armstrong.

He nudges me back.

• • •

In the cabin, with our duffles mostly packed, I'm ready for bed in the top bunk. I'm about to close my eyes when I hear a walkie-talkie squawk under my pillow.

I pick up the receiver and listen.

"Sleepy? Over."

It's Shelley.

"Not really," I say. "Over."

"Me either," she says. "Over."

"Where are you?" I ask. "Over."

"My cabin. Over."

"How'd you get the other . . . ?"

I lean over the side of the bunk. Armstrong's bed is empty. I look back at my walkie-talkie. I press the talk button. There's a little silence while I think of something to say.

"I didn't know you were so good at archery. Over."

"There are a lot of things you don't know about me, Charlie. Over."

"Tell me one," I say. "Over."

"I'm crazy for swimming. When I'm in the water, I feel totally free. Over."

"I feel the same way on skis. Tell me another. Over."

"I can solve a ninth-grade-level crossword puzzle. Over."

"So can I. With a dictionary."

"That's cheating, Rules Boy. Over."

"Hey, I break them sometimes. Tell me one more. Over."

"I left my spinner in the shed. Over."

"Want help finding it? Over?"

"Yes. Over and out."

Armstrong

On my way back into our cabin, I pass Ross coming out. I hand him his flashlight.

"If you get the opportunity," I say, "it's okay to touch tongues."

He nods and starts to go. I tug on his jacket sleeve.

"Don't bite down, though. They don't like that."

He nods again and starts to go, then turns back and hands me his walkie-talkie.

"Hey, Armstrong. Thanks."

"It ain't nothing," I tell him.

"It's something to me," Ross says.

I watch him and his pool of light disappear down the path. And I wonder, is Charlie Ross going to get his first French kiss?

Charlie

Inside the shed, Shelley drapes her red bandanna over my flashlight. It keeps the light low, which is a good thing because I don't want her to see how nervous I am.

There's no bottle to spin, so it's up to me, not chance, to kiss her. I could just tap her on the shoulder, and when she turns around, meet her with a kiss. Or I could ask her if she wants to play seven minutes in heaven. But is that the kind of game you *ask* a girl to play? Or is it like spin-the-bottle, a game that a group plays and you just hope you and your crush end up in heaven at the same time?

"Found it," Shelley says, scooping up her milk-carton spinner.

"Should we head back now?" I ask.

"You want to?"

I shake my head no.

"Me either," she says, smiling.

She looks at me, looks away, looks back again. "You know, Charlie," she says, "you don't have to spin for me anymore."

"I don't?"

"You can just kiss me."

"I wasn't sure when would be the, you know, right time."

Shelley takes hold of my wrist and presses the light on my Timex watch. Four numbers appear in the darkness: 10:03.

"That's as good a time as any."

I put my finger near her face and start tapping her nose, her cheeks, and her chin.

"You've got a funny way of kissing a girl, Charlie Ross."

"I'm counting your freckles first."

She closes her eyes and lets me count. When I get to forty-six, which is all I can find, I whisper the number in her ear.

Then I kiss her.

On the cheek.

She asks if this means she won't have to chase me on the schoolyard anymore and I say yes, but only if she agrees to go steady, and she says yes, so we kiss again, this time on the lips.

I feel something warm and slippery trying to push my lips apart. I think she's trying to French me.

I've never Frenched anyone before. Once, accidentally, I Frenched a dog. I was letting him lick my face, and he must've smelled the tuna from the sandwich I'd eaten, so his tongue went looking for it, and it touched mine. It was a split second, that's all.

I'm trying to keep thoughts of that dog out of my head because this is an actual girl whose tongue is trying to open my lips and I have to decide, am I going to let her or not? I'll bet when I climb into the top bunk tonight, Armstrong is going to ask me if we touched tongues. He'll probably wake the whole cabin with a loud "Sorry-ass chump!" if the answer is no.

Too bad for the cabin. The answer's going to be no.

We kiss some more and then we just hug until we fall asleep, Shelley with her head against my shoulder, me with my head against the wall. I'm not sure how long it is before I hear, "Ross. Ross, you there?"

I look up at the window, half expecting to see him grinning at me. But he's not there.

"Ross, can you hear me? Over."

The walkie-talkie. Shelley must have brought it with her to the shed, to give back. It's in her jacket pocket.

I reach in and pull it out.

Through the speaker I hear a whisper in somebody else's voice.

"Wake up."

Keith's voice.

"What do you want with me?" Armstrong whispers.

"A walk outside. Then a talk. Randy and Tim'll help you out of your bunk."

Shelley and I look at each other, then hurry out of the shed. She holds the walkie-talkie while I anxiously tap the side of my flashlight. We left it on for more than an hour; the batteries are almost dead.

We huddle close and listen for Armstrong's voice on the walkie-talkie.

Nothing. I turn up the volume. Just static. Where are they taking him?

Then I hear Keith's voice over the walkie.

"Didn't your parents teach you not to kiss another guy's girl?"

"How was I supposed to know she was your girl? It's not

like she was wearing a ring or even your shells around her neck."

"She's white. That's ring enough for you. Now, take your hands out of your pockets. I want this to be a fair fight."

"You want to fight me fair? Out here in front of this big old pine tree, the one near the creek about a hundred yards from the boys' cabins? That what you want?"

The walkie-talkie cuts out.

"I'll go for help," Shelley says.

"Take the flashlight."

She bangs it against her thigh. The beam brightens just enough to light her way.

Armstrong

I bet Ross shut off that walkie-talkie 'cause he wanted some privacy. Well, he got his privacy and I'm about to get my ass kicked. Randy and Tim are holding back my arms, and Keith sounds ready to rumble.

Three against one. How is that a fair fight?

"Look here, Keith," I say. "If you really want to fight, let's do it man-to-man. But three to one hardly seems fair."

"Okay," Keith says. "We'll go one at a time. You can save me for last."

The moon is up and just bright enough for me to see where the ground is level and where it drops off toward the creek. Bright enough to see the look on Keith's face. A look that says he's not playing.

Then I hear some gravel sliding down the hill. Somebody's coming. It better be Charlie Ross.

"Keith, man, what's goin' on?"

It's Ross, all right, but his voice sounds funny to me. Like it's him and not him just the same.

"Hey, Charlie Ross. We're about to do a little outdoor education of your friend."

"He's not my friend."

"He's not?"

I'm not?

"He went for your girl, Keith. That crossed the line."

"Good. Good, Charlie Ross. Then you can help with the lesson."

Randy and Tim tighten up on my arms. Keith starts tossing his flashlight into the air and letting it flip over once before catching it again. Seems like everything he touches got to be a weapon.

"Charlie Ross gets the first ten hits," Keith says.

Now I'm starting to wonder what's up with Ross. I went to a lot of trouble arranging that date for him in the shed. This is how he's going to thank me?

Well, here comes another gift from Armstrong Le Rois. I hock a loogie, a real thick one, and unload it right in his face.

"Come on, whitey, kick my ass if you something."

Our eyes latch together. His left one twitches. At least I

think it was a twitch. Might've been a wink.

If it *was* a wink, that's my cue to start playing. Means Ross heard my call for help over the walkie-talkie, and we're about to have one ugly, maybe even bloody, *pretend* fight.

On the other hand, if it was a twitch, it's four to one.

"You think you got something to give? Wake me when you're done."

Charlie Ross thumps me in the chest. I smile. It must've been a wink.

"Harder, Charlie Ross," Keith says.

Here comes another soft white punch.

"You punch all floppy, like your mama's titty," I taunt.

"Are you talking about my mother?" he says, voice all proper and pronouncing every last syllable. It was a wink, for sure.

"Just making a comparison," I say.

He slams his fist into my stomach. That one felt authentic. I hunch over.

"One," Keith says.

Ross pounds me on the shoulder. Maybe it *was* a twitch.

"Two."

"Kick him!"

He kicks me in the shin like it's the start of a football game. I feel a pop of pain and now I know it wasn't a wink. That Charlie Ross! He double-crossed me!

"Three."

He comes in close, egged on by the other boys. Slaps me across the face. Shoves his knee in my gut. I see what it is. He's fixing to pay me back for that time I knocked the wind out of him.

"Four. Five."

Down comes a fist onto my back. Ain't no love tap, neither.

"Six!"

I crumple to the ground. Ross sets his foot on my spine. Looks me all mean in the eye. There goes that twitch again. Or is it a wink now? Honestly, I can't tell.

"What number we up to?" he asks.

"That was seven," Keith says. "But I'll take it from here."

There's a little pause.

"I've got three more coming," Ross says.

"You softened him up for me. Now it's my turn."

"No. You can have what's left of him when I'm done."

Ross raises his foot above my head. I look up at him, trying to read the intention on this boy's face. If it was a twitch, then I'm scared what Ross might do. He puts his foot against my jaw to keep it pressed to the ground.

"Anybody wearing a belt?" he says.

"What do you need a belt for?" Keith asks.

"To finish the lesson."

Out of the corner of my eye, I see Randy lift his shirt and unhook his silver-buckled belt. He pulls it off and hands it to Ross.

Charlie

"Three more coming, Charlie Ross. Make 'em count."

I step back and swing the belt around and around. The buckle whistles in the cold air.

Deep down, so far you can't always see it, there's a lot of courage in you. That comes from the lion inside. But most times, you want everybody to like you, so your lion stays in its den.

I swing the belt toward Armstrong's body. At the last second I change course. The buckle lands with a horrible crack against the side of Keith's head.

The lion is out of its den.

Keith staggers back. His flashlight hits the ground.

My hand shoots down and grabs on to Armstrong. I pull him to his feet.

"Damn, Ross," he says. "You need to learn the difference between a wink and a twitch."

Keith picks up the flashlight and aims it at his own face. Blood drips from his head onto the plastic window in front of the bulb.

"You missed, Charlie Ross," he says.

"No, I didn't."

Keith raises the flashlight above his head. "Stickin' up for *him*? You stupid punk. You deserve this."

He moves toward me waving the light. Randy and Tim step back.

"What the hell are you doing, Keith?" Tim says. "Let's just forget this."

Keith turns to me.

"No. Charlie Ross, I won't ever forget this. Neither will you."

He comes at me swinging the light like a heavy club.

And then everything changes. Out of nowhere comes a thing of blazing speed and blunt force. It whips around and lands on the side of Keith's head, knocking him to the ground —and knocking the flashlight out of his hand.

It's Armstrong's kick.

I bend down and grab the light. I shine it in Keith's face.

"He can kiss whoever he wants," I say. "And it wasn't gross at all. It was nice. They were holding hands."

I throw down the belt and the flashlight and walk past Otis and Cody and Mrs. Gaines and Mr. Mitchell and Mrs. Valentine, who are all standing under the tree now, with Shelley and Jodie.

I walk back to the cabin, alone.

INCIDENT REPORT

Submitted by: Edwina Gaines, Yard Supervisor at Wonderland Avenue School

Date of Incident: Thursday, March 6, 1975

Time: 10:40 p.m.

Location: Clear Creek Outdoor Education Center

Shelley Berman came to the teachers' cabin and said there was about to be a fight down by the river. I gathered up the staff—Mr. Mitchell, Mrs. Valentine, and Counselor Cody—and we raced with our flashlights outside and down to the water. There I saw a boy from the Carpenter School on his knees in front of Charlie Ross. This boy had a gash on the side of his head. Evidently, the Carpenter boys had dragged Armstrong out of his bunk with the intention of doing him harm. His crime? Kissing a white girl. As Yard Supervisor, I feel that adults bear responsibility for this incident. Why weren't there teachers in the boys' bunks after lights out? And what sorts of parents go on teaching skin hatred to their children?

As to the violence, the worst of it was done by Charlie to the Carpenter boy. But it was done in defense of one who was being singled out and ganged up on. I therefore recommend that no punitive action be taken against Armstrong and Charlie.

Armstrong

"You didn't touch tongues."

We're on the bus ride home, everybody so quiet I can hear the tires buzzing on the road. My spot next to Ross has been *supplanted,* which means "taken," by Shelley. They got the armrest pulled up and their hands laced together in her lap. She's leaning on his shoulder, sleeping off the long night we just had. He's leaning on the window, watching the road unwind down the mountain.

"How would you know?"

"I got eyes."

"You spied on us?"

"Nope. I'm spying on you now."

"And what do you see?"

"I see you staring out that bus window, all dreamy. But that's not what tells me you didn't touch tongues with Shelley."

"What tells you?"

"The thing I don't see—your smile in the reflection of that glass."

"How do you know I'm not just being contemplative?"

"Look here, Ross, when a boy gets his first French kiss, he leaves them long words in the dictionary. Talking about *contemplative* . . . If you'd touched tongues, you'd be contemplating how fine it was, and there'd be a dimple-to-dimple grin across your face."

"Well, Mister Le Rois," Ross says, "if you're so sure I didn't French Shelley, then you're right. I didn't."

"I know."

"Want to know why?"

"Yes, I do."

"I'm saving it."

"For what?"

"Andy died two weeks before sixth-grade graduation. He told me he was planning to French-kiss Kathy, his girl-friend. But he never got the chance."

"So you're waiting until you pass him in age?"

"That's right."

"But, Ross, what if we get in a bus crash and you die before your first French kiss? Think of the lost opportunity."

"Then I'll have gotten as far as my brother, and what's wrong with that? Now, if you don't mind, Armstrong, I'd like to go back to looking out the window."

I sit back in my seat and think about Charlie Ross and what he's doing for his brother.

And what he did for me.

"Say, Ross . . ."

"What?"

"You know you're all right, for a white boy."

"I am?"

"You stood up for me out there. Most folks would've sided with their own."

"I did side with my own," he says.

Now it's my turn to be contemplative.

· 15 ·

TEN SATURDAYS

Charlie

I HAVEN'T FORGOTTEN — and neither has my dad — the ten Saturdays of labor I owe him to get my bike out of jail. So, on the first Saturday after Clear Creek at exactly nine a.m., he delivers me to the back of his store.

"Will you be working today too?" I ask.

"I've got a game up at the Club, Charlie. I'll be back at three to pick you up. Until then, Nate's your boss."

He hands me my bagged lunch and drives away.

Saturdays are quiet days at Ross Rents. The store is open only from nine to three, and the phone lines don't light up like crazy the way they do all week long. Gwynne, a skinny woman with long red nails that click the keys of her type-writer, works up front, answering calls when they come and catching up on paperwork for the week ahead. Nathaniel works in back, repairing equipment and getting orders ready for the trucks to deliver on Monday.

I polish the wheelchairs, spray WD-40 into squeaky spots, and think a lot about why I'm here. The kid who followed Keith down Laurel Canyon feels like a stranger to me now.

Nate puts on the radio. "Shining Star," an Earth, Wind & Fire song, plays. He drags a couple of wheelchairs out from their slots, checks an order form on his clipboard, and then brings out a rollaway.

"Ever sleep on one of those?" I say.

"No, Charlie, I never have."

"Consider yourself lucky. I slept on one last Friday. Would've been better off on the floor."

"What was wrong with your regular bed?"

"Occupied," I say, "by Armstrong. He killed me at rugby hoops, so I had to sleep on the rollaway."

Nate smiles, writes a serial number on the order form, then tapes the form to the bed.

"Armstrong slept over?"

I tell him about the field trip to Clear Creek and how the kids from Armstrong's neighborhood needed places to stay the night before.

"Must've been nice to have another boy around."

A fourth person at the table. Laughter in the house. Someone to talk to about Andy.

"Yeah," I say. "It really was."

Nate pulls the next invoice from the stack. He grabs a

dolly and wheels it over to a row of green oxygen tanks. They look like oversize bowling pins.

"I hope someday you go over to his house too, Charlie. Then the circle will come all the way around."

He slides the dolly under a tank and wheels it over to the loading bay.

Armstrong

After Clear Creek we bring home report cards. Daddy looks mine over, says it's better than he ever did, and hands it to Mama, who's especially proud of my A+ in reading. But Lenai spots something they didn't see. In the "Attitudes and Behavior" section under "Shows self-control," they've checked me as "Needs to improve."

"Why don't you take this over and show Mr. Khalil?" Lenai says. Parent Number Three.

On the way there, I fold up my report card like it's a paper football or an airplane. That way Mr. Khalil will see only the parts I want to show.

It's early on Saturday so I use my key. I go inside, say hello to Patches, and call out to the house.

"Mr. Khalil, it's Armstrong. I brought you my report card."

No answer.

I go into the kitchen and see he left the stove on. I shut it off for him.

"Mr. Khalil, you up?"

Long silence. Finally his voice calls back from down the hall. "I'm in the bathroom, Armstrong. Be out in . . . fifteen minutes."

Fifteen is a lot of minutes. I guess at his age things take their time.

It's quiet for one of the fifteen. Then Mr. Khalil says, "Did you say you brought your report card?"

"I did."

"Slide it under the door. I'm low on reading material."

Only trouble with that is, what if he unfolds it, like a newspaper? I walk down that hall praying that he won't.

"Here you go."

I slide the report card under, then lean against the wall to pray some more.

I live with seven people and one bathroom. I know the sounds people make when they're in there. You got your happy sounds, surprised sounds, sounds of struggle, and sounds of relief.

But honestly, right now with Mr. Khalil looking at my report card, I can't tell which is which.

"Ahhhhh," he says, and I hope that's for my grade in reading.

"Hmmmm." That might be the "Needs to improve" in self-control.

Here comes an "OH!" which could be part of the digestive process, or he just found my social studies grade.

Long silence. Followed by a flush.

I hear the sink running. Then just dripping. Then Mr. Khalil opens the door.

"It says you don't always respect authority."

I guess he unfolded it.

"Do I have to respect authority if authority doesn't respect me?"

Mr. Khalil thinks about that. His bushy white eyebrows come together, then apart.

"No," he says. "No, you don't."

He flips over my report card. "But a C in social studies?"

"You're the one who told me about the conscientious objectors to Vietnam. Well, I've been conscientious-objecting to social studies. I don't like how the Indians got killed by the white people. It's not pretty."

"Who says the history of this country is supposed to be pretty?"

"Fine. Maybe it's got some ugliness to it. But Mr. Mitchell's idea of teaching is to make us memorize names. Father this. Junípero that. It doesn't matter to me."

"Everything matters, Armstrong. The way groups of people treat one another. That's history. The way a ball bounces on the ground and rolls a certain way. That's physics. The way friendships are built and sometimes broken. That's humanity.

And the way time moves forward and back inside a person's head. That's memory."

"Okay, I'll work harder in social studies. But otherwise . . . ?"

"Otherwise . . . it's a report card to make a boy proud."

Charlie

After work one Saturday, I'm alone on the driveway when I hear Kathy's skateboard sliding down Greenvalley Road. This time she stops, kicks up her board, and comes to say hi.

It's a little awkward because we haven't talked in almost a year. I ask her how she likes junior high. She's at Bancroft, where I'll start in September.

"It's crowded and there are gym clothes and you have to take showers at PE because kids in junior high sweat a lot. I miss the trees at Wonderland. Math with Miss Sasaki is terrifying. Sewing class is a waste of time. Jazz band is fun, though. I'm learning the saxophone. But I get nervous in front of a crowd."

Her skateboard has an STP decal that's curling up. She tries a couple times to flatten it down, but it won't stick. I get the feeling she's nervous right now.

"There's this friend of mine from the band," she says. "An eighth grade boy. He plays piano. Asked me if I want to see a movie sometime."

"That's nice," I say.

She looks up from her skateboard. "I didn't want to say yes until I asked you."

"Me? What for?"

"Andy and I never broke up."

I hadn't thought of that. When someone dies, if you were going steady, you kind of still are.

"You want me to break up with you? For Andy?"

"Is that weird?"

Not really, I think. How can you go steady with someone who's gone?

"The eighth-grader who plays piano. What's his name?"

"Tyler."

"Go see a movie with Tyler, Kathy. It's what Andy would want. And if he's ever over at your house, bring him by, okay? I'd like to meet him."

"Thank you, Charlie."

She leans forward and gives me a kiss on the cheek. Her hair smells like eucalyptus trees. Like the fort she and Andy made.

I start to count time in twisties. Every Saturday morning my dad drops me at the back of the store. Every Saturday afternoon, when we hear the friendly toot of his horn, Nathaniel walks me out to the alley. He gives my dad a progress report, and as long as I've done a "man's job," I get paid with a twisty from the Alligator Baggies in our kitchen. When we pull into the garage, I tie the twisty onto the spokes of my hanging bike. As soon as I reach ten twisties, my bike will be free.

The closer I get to ten, the closer I get to Shelley, too. After school we meet behind the main school building and make out on the hill under the oak tree. Some days we kiss for thirty seconds at a time, others for two minutes or more. Once, we fell asleep kissing and didn't wake up until it was almost dark and we were drooling.

We still haven't Frenched, though.

One day, after I've earned seven twisties and Shelley and I have recorded our longest kiss yet—twelve minutes and fifty-two seconds, according to my Timex—she tells me I counted wrong.

"You counted forty-six freckles that night in the shed. There's one more."

"There is?"

She turns her head and shows me the back of her earlobe. There's a tiny dot there, like she had her ear pierced only partway through.

I reach out and flick a tree bug from her shoulder. Then I draw a backwards *C,* pushing Shelley's hair behind her ear. My finger touches her forty-seventh freckle.

We kiss again, and right away I feel her tongue against my lips.

"Don't you want to, Charlie?"

"I want to."

She tries again. I pull back.

"Just not yet."

Shelley folds her arms across her chest and looks down.

"Is it my breath?"

"Your breath smells like candy."

"Is it 'cause I'm not cute like Leslie?"

"You *are* cute. And smart. Ninth-grade-crossword-puzzle smart."

She looks at me with her peppermint green eyes.

"I want to wait until I'm a little older," I say.

Shelley scooches away from me. "You're just saying that to be nice." She slides down the hill on her butt.

"Shelley, wait! That's not true!"

Great—now I made a girl cry.

Armstrong

Nobody ever said love is easy. If you ask me, this is all Otis's fault. He should've never put those two together. Now Ross is dragging around a heavy heart, and I'm the one got to lift it up.

"There's plenty of signs in the zodiac, Ross," I say. "Why not try your luck with a Gemini or a Pisces? Otis knows all the girls' signs. Ask him to set you up."

"I don't want to be set up. I want to stay with Shelley."

"Even if it means having to break your promise about Andy?"

He sighs like air leaking from a ball.

"Want me to tell you about *my* first French kiss?"

"Not really."

"It was fourth grade. Amber Williams. Her mama told us to keep an eye on the chocolate chip cookies in the oven. We damn near set the house on fire."

"Fourth grade? You Frenched a girl in fourth grade?!"

"*I* was fourth grade. She was seventh. And, Ross, you should see her now! You will, too, when you come over to my house someday. I know what time in the evening she gets undressed."

"That's not right, spying on a girl."

"This is from the boy who showed me a hole in the wall?"

Ross elbows me in the arm. I elbow him back.

"But seriously, you think you could stay at my place one night like I stayed at yours?"

"I don't see why not. As soon as I'm done with all these Saturdays at Ross Rents, I'll ask my mom and dad."

It'd be nice to introduce Charlie Ross to my family. And to old Mr. Khalil.

Charlie

On my tenth Saturday at Ross Rents, my father's wheelchairs shine as bright as his whitewalls. Nathaniel declares me a first-rate assistant and says he'll report high marks to my dad. But my dad is late to pick me up, and Nathaniel's son is the center fielder in an all-star game this afternoon. Gwynne left ten minutes ago; now Nate has to leave too.

"It's okay, Nathaniel," I say. "He'll be here any minute. I can wait on my own."

"You won't ride around in the electric wheelchairs, will you?"

"Oh, no. Too risky."

"All right, then. You tell your father you did a man's job today."

"I will."

He gives me a wink and heads out back.

As soon as I hear Nathaniel's El Dorado drive off down the alley, I hop on a lightweight Everest & Jennings electric wheelchair and start joy-riding around the store.

I'm doing full-throttle figure eights in the show room, having so much fun that I ignore what might be my father's honk from the back alley. Or it might be somebody else's. The hum of the battery-operated motor makes just enough noise for me to overlook a second honk too.

But then I hear the family signal. In the navy, besides being a celebrated baker, Marty Ross was a radioman, third class, and spent much of his time sending and receiving Morse code. After the war, he brought his dahs and dits back with him to civilian life. They gave us the "rally call of the family," as he put it. In the station wagon on our first trip to

Mammoth, he told Andy and me that we should always ski on the buddy system—nobody goes off alone. "But in case someone does get lost, we'll have a signal, a whistle, that'll help us find each other fast."

He puckered up, and out came a sound like a bird in a forest: *twah twooh twooh, twooh twah twah twooh, twooh twah twooh twooh, twah twah.*

"What's it mean?" Andy had asked.

"It's Morse code. *Dah dit dit, dah dah dit dit, dah dah dit dit dah dah.* A call for all ships to return to port. And it'll serve us well as a family signal—if you're lost in a crowd, just listen for my whistle. A whistle travels farther than a voice."

So does the horn of a car. *Hah honk honk, hah hah honk honk honk, hah hah honk honk hah hah.*

I race the wheelchair back into its slot. *Idiot!* I left the bathroom light on. I walk across the warehouse to turn it off, then head back and push open the heavy steel door to the alley.

Where my father is standing outside the car. His hands are on the luggage rack, his back toward me.

Two men stand close behind him. I see my father slowly reach around to his back pocket. He pulls out his wallet. One of the men snatches it from his hand.

The other opens the door and shoves him toward the back seat.

My father doesn't get in. The man pulls something small and dark from his jacket — is it a gun? — and presses it against my father's head.

My whole body starts to shake. I want to speak but my mouth is dry. I want to shout, *Don't hurt my dad! Take his money but don't take him.* I want to say, *He's my dad and I love him, so please don't. Please . . .*

He's kneeling now and crawling into the car.

I can hardly feel my legs. Somehow they carry me into the alley.

No! I think. *Stop!* I want to say. The words are dust in my mouth.

I hear a click. The man's arm points inside the back seat of the car.

NO! I scream. But no sound comes.

I take another step. My shoe crunches a rock. Both men turn their heads to look at me.

"Please," I say. "That's my dad."

The gun is still pointed into the back of the car. The eyes are pointed at me.

Then the gun disappears into the jacket. The men disappear down the alley.

I walk over to the car. The back door is still open. I lean in. "Dad . . ."

He doesn't answer. I move closer. On the floor of the back seat, my father looks as small as a child.

"Dad."

I climb in and lie across the seat above him. I put my hand on his back.

"Dad, it's okay. They're gone now."

He lifts his head to look at me. "Charlie?"

He sits up, and I put my arms around him, and he leans against me, growing back to his full size in my arms. We're there like that, in the back seat of our family car, in the alley behind his store, until I feel my dad take up his own weight again.

We get out and he looks down the alley, up the alley, down the alley and up, like he's trying to piece together what happened. Where those men came from. Why he didn't see them coming.

When he speaks, his voice sounds like it's behind a mask.

"Your mother mustn't know about this, Charlie," he says. "She's had enough to deal with this year. We can't add one more thing. Do you understand?"

I nod.

"You won't speak about it to her. To anyone. Do I have your word, Charlie, that you'll never speak about this to anyone?"

"Yes, Dad," I say. "You have my word."

Armstrong

Early on Sunday I head over to Mr. Khalil's with my work gloves on. I promised I'd help plant his tomatoes today, and he promised he'd teach me how to make a caramel cake for Mother's Day.

Mr. Khalil is usually up at dawn. He says old people lose the habit of sleeping the closer they get to the grave. They develop what he calls vampire sleep—most of it during the day—so at night they're wide awake, tossing and turning or taking pills to quiet their minds.

"Mr. Khalil," I say, opening up his door with my key. On weekends I've been coming by to help him get the day started. Bring him his newspaper and set the water to boil on his stove. I offered to learn how to make his coffee, but he said I wouldn't make it strong enough. I would if you teach me, I said. But he said no. There are things a man has to do for himself while he still can.

"Mr. Khalil," I say again when the kettle's on. "You want your newspaper in bed?"

There's no answer from the bedroom. He's probably in the bathroom doing his business.

Patches must be outside doing his, too. Mr. Khalil's afternoon naps have been so long, and his afternoon walks so short, we had to put in a doggy door so Patches wouldn't pee in the house. I look out the back window. Patches isn't in the yard.

Then I hear some whining from the bedroom. Sounds like a dog but not like a dog at the same time.

"Mr. Khalil, you awake?"

No answer.

I push open his bedroom door. Patches is there, *rah-rah-ruffin'* at me from the top of the bed, his paws stretched out over Mr. Khalil's chest like he's guarding a toy.

"Patches?" I say. "What in the world—"

All of a sudden I remember that time we stepped in footprints and put our palms in handprints at the Chinese Theatre. Afterward we went to a place called the Hollywood Wax Museum, where you could see life-size copies of famous people made of wax. I remember hiding behind Daddy's leg because I was scared the wax people would jump out and grab me, and their touch would be like the Midas touch, and that's where I'd stay forever, a living boy trapped inside a wax body.

My sisters teased me cruel about it. "Armstrong, those people are as likely to grab hold of you as a dead man is to get up out of his grave."

Well, imagine Ebony's scream when one of them wax figures grabbed hold of her arm. The museum had put a *real* person in with all the wax ones. He jumped out and nearly stopped my sister's heart.

So with wax figures, you never know if they're for real or not.

But with people, you know. Right now Mr. Khalil is

lying in his bed like he's made of wax. I'm scared to get close in case Patches won't let me. But when I take one more step, a half one, into the room, Patches leaps off the bed and comes to me. He shoves his nose into my hand like he always does when he wants some love.

I take another step toward the bed. Mr. Khalil is so peaceful, so still. He could be in a deep sleep from one of those pills he told me about.

I take *another* step and touch his hand. It's cold. I feel for a pulse by his wrist. Nothing there. I sit on the edge of his bed, and I can't help it — my tears start to come.

In the kitchen, the kettle whistles up to a scream. It gets louder and louder, and I think if it gets loud enough, it might wake him.

But my old friend Mr. Khalil will not be waking anymore.

· 16 ·

A THOUSAND FLAGS AWAY

Charlie

EVERY MOTHER'S DAY MORNING, Andy would get up early and go out to the backyard with Dad's clippers and cut the last of the calla lilies on the hill. In midwinter, when they come up from the ground, they stand tall and rolled up tight. Week by week they open into these perfect cone-shaped flowers, white with a bright yellow stick—a spadix, Dad called it —in the center.

"The calla lilies tell time," Andy would say. "It's February when they come up from the ground. March when they start to unroll. April when they're ready for the Passover table. May when just a few are left standing on the hill. June when they fall down."

We were never allowed to cut them before Passover. But when Andy would bring in the last ones for Mother's Day, Mom would say, "Is it May already? This year sure has flown by."

Today is the first Mother's Day without him. I wake up early and go into the garage. It smells of WD-40 and rusty screws, chrome polish, and S.O.S pads. I reach up and grab the clippers off my dad's pegboard.

I'm about to turn and go when I notice the dome light on in his car.

"What's that, boys?" I hear a voice say. "You want me to lie down? Okay, fellas. You'll get no trouble from me. Here you go. My wallet. And my watch. I won't look up before I count to a hundred . . . One, two, three, four . . ."

Inside my father's car, an arm rises up over the back seat, then a head, a shoulder. I see my father climb into the front. He doesn't see me.

"Six . . . seven . . . eight . . ." he counts.

He grabs the steering wheel.

"Nine . . . ten!"

He grips it like a throat.

"Animals! You son of a bitch! I'll run you into the ground!"

He puts his hand on the gearshift and makes like he's putting the car in reverse. He throws his arm over the seat-back, whips his head around, and looks out the rear window.

Then he swings his head around again, pretends to shift back into drive, and says, "Now you!"

Again he grips the wheel with two hands. And he rages, "WHERE'S YOUR GUN NOW, YOU GODDAMNED BAS—"

I cover my ears and pray for it to end.

· · ·

Andy would always cut the flowers, and I would write the note. *Happy Mother's Day to our best friend.* Or *Dear Mom, You never go out of bloom.* Or *Don't worry, we didn't drop the vase. Love, Andy and Charlie.* Or *Love, Your two and only.*

This year I wish I could write *Dear Mom, a terrible thing happened to Dad. He made me promise not to tell. Ask him, okay? He needs your help. Love, Charlie.*

Instead I write *Dear Mom, Happy Mother's Day. Love, Charlie.*

I leave the calla lilies in a vase by her Mr. Coffee machine. That way she'll see them first thing when she comes downstairs.

Armstrong

When my grandma passed, she nearly turned one dead person into nine. We spent three whole weeks going through her boxes of old clothes, stacks of finger paintings from when we were little, post cards she kept from all her friends who had gone, jars of candy, matches from every restaurant where she ate, shoes that her first husband wore, shirts from her second, old records she was too deaf to hear, seashells and sea glass and other bits and pieces she liked to collect on her walks.

If I live to be an old man, I'm going to have a garage sale

every week starting when I turn eighty-five. That way I'll unload before I leave.

Like Mr. Khalil did. Other than his clothes, he left just one box of papers, some tools, and all those books. His library's the one thing he held on to all his life.

"How in the world did that man find time to read all these?" Cecily asks.

"When you live to ninety-five," my daddy says, "you're blessed with a lot of time."

We stand there looking up at his shelves. Must be close to a thousand books here.

"What are we going to do with all these?" Ebony says.

"Can I keep a few?" Charmaine says.

"Can I?" Nika says.

"I want some," Lenai says.

"Me too," from Cecily.

"You'll have to ask Armstrong," my daddy says. "They're his now."

Mine?

"Armstrong," Mama says, "we have something to tell you. Something to read to you."

She looks at my daddy. He lifts a folder from Mr. Khalil's desk and reads aloud from a letter.

"I, Solomon Khalil, of Los Angeles, California, being of sound mind and memory, and not acting under duress or fraud, do hereby make, publish, and declare this my

*last will and testament. First, I direct that all my just
debts and funeral expenses be paid. Second, I nominate
my attorney, Stuart Friedman, as executor of this will.
Third, I give and bequeath unto my friend, Armstrong
Le Rois, a minor, all the contents of my home, including
my books and my dog, Patches, with the request that
he read the books and look after the dog. Fourth, I
give and bequeath unto the executor the proceeds of
my estate, to be placed in trust for the use and benefit
of Armstrong Le Rois, and to be used in the following
manner: All proceeds shall be invested in a fund for
the exclusive purpose of paying for Armstrong's college
education. Upon his graduation from a college or
university, any remaining funds shall be used to pay for
his pursuit of an advanced degree, if he so desires, or be
held in trust for him until he attains the age of thirty,
at which time the balance shall be paid over to him. In
witness whereof, I have here set my hand.*

Solomon Khalil."

"Does this mean Armstrong is going to be rich?"

"No. It means Armstrong is going to go to college."

"And he's got himself a dog."

I reach out and take the letter from my daddy's hand into mine. I bring it close to my face, and the whole world disappears except for that letter. I read it again and again.

Some of the words jump out like flowers you might see in a time-lapse film. *Give and bequeath . . . Armstrong Le Rois . . . college education . . . trust . . . benefit . . . friend.*

The words go out of focus from the tears in my eyes.

Charlie

I'm not allowed in the living room tonight. It's Mom's turn to host the consciousness-raising group.

But I *am* allowed to sneak a chocolate-chip roll from the platter in the dining room. And I would have gone straight back upstairs without stopping if I hadn't just heard Kay Kahn tell the group that her husband, Harry, "has been depressed lately."

She says his business has slowed down. She says he won't talk about it with her. All through dinner, all night long, the only voices she hears come from the TV or the kids.

"Marty hasn't been himself either," my mom says. "It's almost a year since we lost Andy. I think he's finally starting to grieve."

"Does he talk about him?" Annette DeWitt asks.

"He talks about his business. He talks about numbers. But not about our son."

I wish I could say something. I wish I hadn't promised not to tell.

Armstrong

Monday morning I find Ross and tell him what I've been waiting all weekend to tell.

"Guess what I got?"

No guess.

"It has a tail."

Still no guess.

"One that wags when I get home from school."

Still no guess.

"A dog, silly."

"That's nice." His tone says he doesn't care.

"Don't you want to know how come I got this dog?"

"Huh?"

"I say, don't you want to know how come I got this dog?"

"If you want to tell me."

"It's part of my inheritance. From old Mr. Khalil."

"Who?"

"The man I've been looking after. I told you about him, remember?

"Oh, yeah."

Ross seems like he didn't get much sleep last night.

"Well, the thing is, he died over the weekend."

Now Charlie Ross looks at me like I got his attention.

"For real this time?"

"For real this time. Had a heart attack in his sleep. But don't worry — he fed the dog first."

"I'm sorry, Armstrong."

"Everyone says he was ninety-five. Lived a good life. But it still hurts to lose a friend."

If anybody should know about that, it's Charlie Ross. Man, what was I thinking that time I paid him no respect about his brother? Earlier this year Mr. Mitchell asked us to write about a time machine. If we could go back to any time in history, where would we go? I said back to when the first humans appeared in Africa so I could prove that all people came from black people. But now I'd like to change my answer to that day in the bathroom with Charlie Ross. Have what my daddy calls a do-over.

"His name is Patches, by the way."

"Huh?"

"The dog. Probably named for his missing fur. He's my responsibility now. And he's real friendly, Ross, especially to boys. I think you're going to like him when you meet him next Friday."

"Next Friday?"

"That's when my mama and daddy said you can come sleep over at our house, *if* it's okay for you to be out on Shabbat."

"We're not that religious," Ross says.

"Good. Oh, and do you like pancakes? I found a recipe that Mr. Khalil handwrote in a little book of his. I'm going to fix 'em for you. But we'll have to be up early or my sisters'll eat the whole batch."

"I have to ask my parents."

"Ask 'em soon, okay?"

"I will," he says in a robot voice.

Maybe Charlie Ross doesn't care for dogs.

Charlie

Would it be safe in his neighborhood? Would it be safe to even ask my dad?

Armstrong

"Say, Ross, you ask your parents about coming over to my house?"

"Not yet," he says, "but I will."

I ask him again the next day.

"Not yet," he says, "but I will."

And the day after that.

"Not yet," he says, "but I will."

We're running out of days.

Charlie

Thursday night at dinner, Mom asks the question that Dad used to ask every night but hasn't asked once since what happened in the alley behind Ross Rents. "What stood out for you about this day, Charlie?"

I tell her not much because it's the truth. We've gotten all the way to Finland in geography and all the way to gold in the SRA box. In math, even Jason can multiply fractions now. We're all pretty much ready for junior high.

I look over at my dad. His eyes are on his plate.

Finally, to stop the silence, I say, "Mom, Dad, Armstrong wanted me to ask you if I can sleep over at his house next Friday."

Mom starts to say, "I don't see why not," but the "not" runs into my dad.

"I'm afraid that isn't such a good idea, Charlie," he says. "Armstrong lives in a rough neighborhood. It wouldn't be safe for you to be there at night."

He gives me a look that's just between us.

Armstrong

"There goes Houdini's house."

"Hou-what?"

"Houdini."

We're on the way to school, waiting to turn from Laurel Canyon onto Lookout Mountain. Otis just leaned forward and tapped me on the shoulder.

"Who was he?"

"Only the greatest master of magic that ever was. And that's the house where he lived *after* he died."

I look at Otis with one of my eyebrows up and the other one down. The logic of that just doesn't make sense.

"It's true," Otis says. "I've been reading about it in this book I got from the library."

He holds up *Haunted Hollywood: Ghostly Encounters.*

Looks like Otis is moving on from astrology.

"What's it say?"

"It says Houdini used to do all kinds of magic tricks. And for his last one, he told his wife, Bess, that if there was any way to come back from the dead, he would do it. Right there in that house."

I've been thinking about ghosts lately. Yesterday I went over to Mr. Khalil's yard and was twisting weeds until I heard the roots crack, and when I looked up, on the porch I swear I saw old Mr. Khalil watching me work. His head was nodding like he approved of the job. Later on, I was in the bathroom washing my hands. I looked in the mirror, and right behind me was Mr. Khalil. I spun around. But he was gone.

"Well, did he?" I ask Otis.

"Did he what?"

"Come back from the dead."

"I'm only on page forty-five. I'll let you know when I finish the book."

Before school I step into the boys' bathroom and find Ross at the sink, staring at himself in the mirror like he's in some kind of trance. Got the water running, but his hands hang down by his side.

I shut the water off. "You okay?"

He shrugs his shoulders. Something's wrong with this boy. Something's been wrong with him for a whole week.

"Everything okay with Shelley?"

He nods his head.

"Everything okay with Charlie?"

There goes that shrug again.

"Say, did you remember to ask your parents?"

He nods.

"And?"

"I can't come."

"You can't?"

"My dad said no."

I feel a swirl inside my belly.

"He say why?"

"Just that we're busy."

"All the way to June?"

"All the way to June."

Charlie

It's what my mom would call a white lie. You tell a white lie when you don't want to hurt someone's feelings.

Armstrong

On Saturday I walk over to Mr. Khalil's garden. I'm going to plant those tomatoes. It's late for tomatoes, but maybe I'll get lucky.

I miss him sitting on the porch and telling me what to do.

I miss talking to him.

I'd like to ask him, did he ever have a friendship turn cold?

Charlie

The problem with telling a white lie is that you keep the truth all to yourself. But what if it's a truth you have to tell?

Monday on the basketball court, I make sure to take

four steps on the way to a lay-up. It's so obvious I was traveling, even Alex sees it. The shot goes in.

Armstrong gets the ball and goes to take it out.

"Didn't you see that extra step?"

"I saw it."

"Why didn't you call traveling, then?"

"Figured someone else would."

"But no one did. They depend on you, Armstrong."

"What's that mean, Ross?"

"You're the captain. Always have been. If you don't make the call, who will?"

"It doesn't matter if I make the call."

"It *does* matter. I'm the Rules Boy, remember?"

"You got your set of rules. I got mine."

"No. They're the same set of rules."

"You're a dumb white boy if you think they are."

"Come over to my house again, Armstrong."

"You come over to mine."

"I told you I can't."

"Same set of rules, huh?"

Armstrong passes the ball hard into my gut. The bell rings, and he walks off the court. I see him heading for the boys' bathroom.

I drop the ball and follow him in.

"There's a reason," I say.

"I know the reason. And I'm a dumb black boy for forgetting it long enough to be your friend."

"It has to do with my dad."

"He's got something against me?"

"Not you."

"Who, then?"

I look away.

"*Who*, then?"

I look into the face of my friend. And I tell the truth I have to tell.

"He was mugged. Two men put a gun to his head. They made him lie down in the back of the car."

Armstrong looks away for a moment. When he looks back, his eyes are full of tears.

"Were they black?" he asks.

I nod.

"I see," he says. "So we're all holding the gun?"

Armstrong

. . .

Charlie

. . .

Armstrong

In class Mr. Mitchell announces a project we have to do. "A relief map of the city of Los Angeles."

I can hardly wait.

Leslie hands out the city maps while Melanie and Alex pass around the art supplies.

"After you mold the mountains and other geographical features, you'll paint them — blue for water, green for flatlands, brown for the hills."

Otis raises his hand. "Can we work in partners?"

"I don't usually like partners work," Mr. Mitchell says. "But we do need to spread out for this project. And we may not have enough supplies. All right, everybody find a partner."

Heads spin. Arms reach across rows. Names bounce from mouth to mouth. Otis pairs up with Alex. Susan Campbell with Shelley. Leslie over by Melanie.

"Hey, Charlie, wanna partner up?" Jason Vale calls from across the room.

Ross pokes me in the arm.

"Partners?" he says.

"Yours is waiting for you over there," I tell him.

Charlie

I make the mountain ranges and Jason figures out where they should go. Just before the bell rings, Mr. Mitchell passes out miniature American flags. He tells us to plant the flag on our map at the exact location of Wonderland Avenue School.

Laurel Canyon is the fourth canyon from downtown. I trace its winding path from Hollywood Boulevard up to Lookout Mountain, then west about a half mile to where Lookout hits Wonderland Avenue. There I raise the American flag.

I look back at the rest of the city, from our Canyon all the way downtown. I remember from the school form that Armstrong lives on Fifty-third Street.

When my dad told me about the Opportunity Busing program last summer, he said the new kids would be coming from a housing development in South Central. *Ninety-nine percent black,* he said. I pictured Armstrong's neighborhood at least fifty miles from here.

I take the flag out of our map and touch the point of the

toothpick to Wonderland. Then, aiming for South Central LA, I move the flag end over end across the city, until it reaches Fifty-third Street.

I measure the distance against our scale. It's around twenty miles.

Across the room, I see Armstrong working alone, a thousand flags away.

Armstrong

Those men who mugged Papa Ross did a terrible thing. But why should that bring shame on us all?

If you look at statistics, white people do a lot more violence than black people. How many brothers in history started a war? How many dropped the atomic bomb? Or killed the Indians? It's mostly white people who've done the nastiest deeds.

Look at that. I just passed a black man on the street, and he didn't mug me. There's two more sitting on a bench. Did they put a gun to my head?

Here comes Otis's grandma on her way to the store.

"Hello, Mrs. Greene. Were you planning to mug me today, ma'am?"

"Stop talking nonsense, Armstrong!"

She walks on with her cane.

I'm going to count the number of black people who don't mug me just to show Charlie Ross how crazy it is to fear us all.

Charlie

I was wrong about the distance to Armstrong's house. It's more like fifteen miles.

Armstrong

"Say, Ross," I tell him the next morning before school, "know how many black people I passed yesterday?"

"No."

"Forty-two. Know how many put a gun to my head?"

"How many?"

"Zero."

That's all I've got to say to Charlie Ross today.

Charlie

"Is it because he's black?"

"What?"

Dad's in the driveway, washing Mom's car. She's been going out more often lately. You can tell by the whitewalls.

I walk over to the bucket and lift out the sponge. I start soaping up the hood.

"Is that why you don't want me to go over to Armstrong's house?"

"I told you, it's the neighborhood. Crime rates are higher down there."

Dad dips the pad in sudsy water, wrings it out, and scrubs some more. Then he stops and looks at me.

"I can't help it, Charlie. Now when I see a black man coming toward me, my heart beats fast. My hands turn to fists. They don't unclench until he's gone."

"But, Dad, you don't feel that way around *all* black people. You don't feel that way around Nathaniel and Gwynne."

"I told you, I'm not comfortable with you going down there. There's nothing more to discuss."

He goes back to scrubbing. All the way through the S.O.S pad to his bare hand.

Friday at lunch, I eat alone. Armstrong eats alone. Shelley eats at a table with Alma and Dezzy. I wait for her to crumple up her bag and throw it away.

"Can I talk to you?" I ask.

"Talk," she says.

I glance over to the secret path behind the building, where we used to disappear together to be alone.

Under our oak tree, I tell Shelley about what I saw happen to my dad and what it's been doing to Armstrong and me. She doesn't say anything, just listens. But when I get to the end, she reaches out and takes my hand. For the rest of lunch, we just sit there like that, holding hands. Sometimes we let go to wipe our palms on our jeans. But then our hands come right back together again.

When the bell rings, Shelley says, "Maybe it's not up to your mom and dad, Charlie. Maybe it's up to you."

After school, the buses are lined up in the yard and the drivers are stretching their legs. I walk past Mr. Orr's small square-backed bus and stand next to the long Crown bus with a rounded back, rumbling engine, and hydraulic brakes. The kind of enormous magical vessel that we only get to ride when there's a field trip.

When nobody's looking, I get on that bus and sneak down the aisle to the last seat. I crouch down and hide.

I'm going on a field trip of my own.

· 17 ·

CHARLIE IN THE HOUSE

Armstrong

AFTER WE PICK UP the Opportunity Busing students at other schools, the bus is loud and full. We're heading down La Cienega to the freeway when I look out like I always do to see if I can spot Papa Ross in the window at Ross Rents. He's there, all right, helping an old man find the right-fitting wheelchair to ride. I lift my hand to wave at him, but he's too busy to see.

On the Santa Monica Freeway we head east toward downtown. Air whistles through the windows. Conversations quiet down. People got their bobble heads on.

One of the high school girls just got mad at the boy behind her. He won't quit playing with her hair. She goes past me on her way to the last seat.

That's when she screams.

"MR. SIMMS, THERE'S A WHITE BOY ON THIS BUS!"

"Say what?"

"There's a white boy on this bus!"

Mr. Simms puts on the hazard lights. He pulls the bus over to the side of the road. A sign says EMERGENCY PARKING ONLY.

Guess whose head pops up from behind the last seat.

"Young man," says Mr. Simms, "I think you're on the wrong bus."

"It's the right one today," Charlie Ross says. "I'm going over to my friend's house for dinner."

"Is your friend on this bus?"

"That's him right there."

He points me out like I'm in a lineup.

"Why aren't you sitting together?"

"We're in a fight," Ross says.

"And you're going over to his house to make up?"

"Yep."

Everybody on the bus laughs. Everybody but me. Then Mr. Simms asks Charlie Ross if has a permission slip from his parents.

"Sure I do," Ross says.

"Let's see."

"Yeah, Ross," I say, "let's see the permission slip from your parents authorizing you to be my friend."

Ross digs into his jeans and pulls out a candy wrapper, a stick of Juicy Fruit, and a dime.

"It was here this morning."

"Maybe you'd better put him off the bus, Mr. Simms,"

one of the boys from Hollywood High says. "Make him walk home on the freeway."

"I'll put him off the bus at Holmes along with the rest of you. Then we'll make a phone call."

Charlie

"What's your phone number?"

We're standing in the office at Armstrong's old school.

"It's 625-3131," I say, my eyes aimed at the countertop.

Mr. Simms dials and gets a busy signal.

Armstrong stands behind me, a thin smile on his face, while the bus driver dials again—and again—and gets the third busy signal in a row.

"I got to get home to my own kids now. You sure they said you could go over to his house?"

"It's no big thing, Mr. Simms," Armstrong says. "We'll call again from my house."

"Tell me that number again."

"It's 625-3131."

He dials one more time. Busy again.

"You walk him straight home now, you hear?"

"I'll run him there, sir."

Mr. Simms goes.

When we're outside, Armstrong says, "You're lucky they're on the phone."

"They're not on the phone," I say. "I gave Mr. Simms the number he was dialing from. Automatic busy signal."

Armstrong can't hide his smile.

Armstrong

It's a ten-minute walk from Holmes Avenue Elementary to my house. I can see Ross's head turning from side to side like he's terrified. The late afternoon sun is making our shadows long. They look like twins, twelve feet tall.

"Look out, Ross. There's a couple of black men."

"Where?"

"Right in front of us. Two tall ones on the sidewalk."

"That's just our shadows."

"Well, you're acting like you're afraid of your own."

I throw my arm around his neck and pull him into a headlock. Our shadows bunch together like a single giant walking on four legs.

Charlie

We come to two rows of two-story apartment buildings facing each other across a dry lawn. Some clotheslines are up with shirts and jeans hanging out to dry. A breeze lifts the sleeve of a sweatshirt. It looks like it's waving hello.

"The buildings all look the same," I say, more or less thinking aloud.

"Oh, now you're being racist about the houses, too."

"I didn't mean—"

"I know what you mean. You think all these project houses look alike. Well, maybe on the first white glance they do. But look at that red shirt hanging out to dry, Ross. That's Amber Williams's favorite T-shirt. I told you I know what time she takes it off in the evening. And see that bike with training wheels? It used to be mine, but we gave it to Kaditha Edwards when her son Brian turned five. That barbecue there belongs to the Taylors. Every Sunday afternoon we can smell what they're having for dinner."

He points to a corner apartment. In the window, I see a barking dog.

"That's Patches. He's not allowed on the couch, but he gets up there anyway to see me come home."

We walk closer to that unit. Armstrong pulls out a key on a cord from under his shirt. He unlocks the door, pushes it open, and kneels to greet his dog.

"Patches!"

Patches wags his tail and licks Armstrong all over the face. But when he sees me on the front step, he starts to growl.

"Quit it, Patches," Armstrong says. "That's Ross and he's all right." To make me feel better, he adds, "He barks at Otis, too."

"Patches is a good boy," I say in my dog voice. He comes up and sniffs my hand. His tail wags, so I step inside.

"We've got two bedrooms. My parents stay in one and my five sisters in the other."

"Where do you sleep?"

"Right here. After nine o'clock, the living room belongs to me. That's my couch-bed, and there's that TV I told you about."

Just then, a voice cracks into the room like a whip.

"Son, get on in the kitchen!"

Patches's tail goes stiff between his legs as a man on crutches steps into the living room from the hall. He's got one leg on the ground. The other one disappears into a flap of fabric on his pants.

"Daddy," Armstrong says, "say hello to Charlie Ross, the boy from my school."

"It's a pleasure to meet you, young Mr. Ross," his father says, "but your friend and I have some business to discuss in the kitchen."

Armstrong leads the way and I follow. Behind us comes the *boom-creak, boom-creak* of his father's step.

In the kitchen Mr. Le Rois stabs one crutch toward an artificial leg leaning against the wall.

"Now go on and say what you see."

"I see your artificial leg, Daddy."

"Say what you see in front of it on the floor."

"I see a puddle of water."

"That's not water."

"Looks like water to me."

"If that's water, why don't you kneel down and drink some?"

"I'm not thirsty."

"Everybody can work up a thirst for a little drink of water. Go on. Lean over and lap it up. Like a dog."

Armstrong crouches in front of the puddle, leans his nose toward it, and sniffs.

"That's not water," he says.

"Know what it is?"

"Urine."

"Yours?"

"No, sir."

"Mine?"

"No, sir."

I can see Armstrong's lip start to quiver, but he doesn't dare laugh.

"Is that a twitch, or you about to bust up at your own daddy?"

"Twitch."

Mr. Le Rois's eyes lock on to his son's.

"It was a twitch, Daddy. I swear."

"Down and give me five, just in case."

Armstrong makes two fists, drops to the floor, and does five pushups on his knuckles. Each one brings his face an inch from the puddle.

"Now, I expect we know whose urine it is, don't we?"

"Yes, sir."

"Patches is his name, that right?"

"Yes, sir."

"Your dog has lifted his leg on mine."

"I'm sorry, Daddy."

"Not half as sorry as you'll be if you don't run along and get the Windex."

Armstrong bolts down the hall to a bathroom, leaving me alone with his dad. Mr. Le Rois stands there leaning on his crutch, studying me with those steel eyes.

"Teddy Le Rois," he finally says, putting out his hand. I shake it and hear my knuckles crack.

"Your father serve in the Korean War?" he asks.

"No, sir," I say. "World War Two. In the navy, sir."

"Wounded?"

"No, sir." I can't help it. He's just the kind of man you have to call sir. "They were on a patrol ship in the Pacific when we dropped the bomb and the war ended."

At this point Armstrong's dad leans forward on his crutch, his face coming into the light over the table, and he looks at me. Practically through me.

"You're wondering about my leg, aren't you?"

I am, but I don't dare admit it.

"I was a commander with the Seventy-seventh Engineering Corps, one of the last all-black divisions in the army. And I can tell you that black or white, new soldier or old, we were all scared. Nobody went to Korea prepared for that. They had the Chinese fighting along with the North Koreans. They came at us by the thousands, came at night while we slept. First with their bugles. Then with their bullets.

"We joined with the Twenty-fourth Infantry at the first American battle victory of the war. Needed to make a bridge across the Yechon River. Me and my boys set to building it, and we were almost to the other side when them bugles started spitting brass. It was an ambush and we didn't have cover. Didn't have reinforcements, either. The enemy lost two hundred fifty-eight men that day. We lost two. Two men and a limb.

"Do you know how many black soldiers were serving in 1950, while we were still segregated?"

"No, sir."

"A hundred thousand."

"Know how many were serving by the end, when they let black and white serve side by side?"

I shake my head.

"Six hundred thousand, many of them volunteers. What's that tell you?"

"People try harder when they're treated the same?"

"Now you know why we sent our boy to your school."

I nod. I know it's more polite to just listen than to ask questions. But there's one thing I've got to know.

"But . . . how do you fight now?"

"I don't. Uniform's hanging in the closet."

"I mean, professionally, sir. In the ring."

"The ring?"

"Aren't you a kickboxer, Mr. Le Rois?"

"A one-legged kickboxer? Whatever gave you that idea?"

Just then, Armstrong comes back with a bottle of Windex and some rags. He kneels down and starts spraying and buffing the floor. His father watches him work.

"Soon as it's dry you can give me twenty-five."

"What for, Daddy?"

"Talking about your daddy is a kickboxer. What in the world is going on in that head of yours?"

Armstrong gives me a look that previews the ass-kicking I'm in for.

Then Teddy Le Rois surprises us both. He sinks to the ground, supporting himself on his knuckles and his one leg, and brings his face level with Armstrong's.

"Let's you and me do them pushups together."

They go down together and come up together, down together and up. After six pushups, Teddy Le Rois says, "You wish I had both my legs, don't you?"

"Yes, sir," Armstrong answers.

"So do I, son. But I'm not sorry I fought for my country. Even if my country doesn't always fight for me. Understand?"

Armstrong nods, and they do a few more pushups. Their eyes never leave each other.

"What am I supposed to put down on the school form? Under 'Father's occupation'?"

"You can put down that I'm the Man of the House."

"That's a job?"

"Yes, it is. It means while your mama's out earning the money we need to live, I'm at home, minding your sisters and you. That's something you can be proud of, Armstrong. At the end of the day, not every boy's got a daddy waiting on the other side of the door."

Mr. Le Rois glances from Armstrong to me.

"What number we up to, Charlie?"

"Twenty, sir," I say.

I count out loud the rest of the way to twenty-five.

· 18 ·

DIFFERENT AND THE SAME

Armstrong

AFTER WE FINISH — and by "we," I mean Ross and me — cleaning the kitchen floor, I take him and Patches for a walk along Fifty-third Street, past the corner store where I bought my Ho Hos, and over to Morgan Avenue. We go by a garden wall that's been painted sky blue and filled with colorful birds.

Ross stops to look. "That's a nice mural," he says.

"You'll have to tell my sister Cecily," I say, "when you meet her."

We walk on some more. Past houses that aren't being looked after and some that are. This one belongs to Mr. and Mrs. Wong. The yard's got daisies and grass and not a single weed.

"Nika and Ebony did the weeding on that one," I say. "And me and Lenai put in those beans across the street." I point to where some beanstalks are coming up.

"You work for those people?"

"I work for myself. The people are my clients, Ross. Here's my card."

I hand him one of the cards Cecily helped me design. My logo is a wheelbarrow full of flowers and tools. Across the top it says ARMSTRONG'S ODDS & ENDS.

"Come on," I say, "I'll show you the best house of all."

Near the end of the block we come to a house with a painted wood fence and a bright garden in front. Good curb appeal. There's an indestructible porch wrapped around that home, and the windows all have fresh caulking so they won't leak. On the south side, where the most sun shines, is a small vegetable garden with young tomato plants, green beans, and kale growing.

"Know whose house this is?" I say.

Ross just shakes his head.

"Mine."

"Yours?"

"Mr. Khalil left it to me. That's why he was training me so hard in maintenance and repairs. My daddy and I are fixing it up so we can rent it out."

Ross is looking at the house like he doubts I'm for real.

"For real?" he says.

I hold up my key.

Charlie

Armstrong unlocks the door and pushes it open. I just stand there, a little awkward because I never met his old friend Mr. Khalil. He might not want a stranger in his house.

But Armstrong says, "Really, Ross, he would want you to come in."

So I follow him inside.

In the living room Armstrong shows me some old black-and-white pictures of Mr. Khalil when he was young. In one he's on a stage and holding up a skull.

"He never had that out when he was alive, but my mama and I found it in this old box he kept. The box had one word on it: THEATER. Inside we saw programs and reviews of the plays he acted in. And he was good, too."

Armstrong opens the drawer of an old wooden table, moves some papers around, then says, "Look at this!"

He holds up a scrap of yellow newspaper with a head-line: "Solomon Khalil Is This Season's Best Hamlet, Uptown or Down."

"After his acting days, Mr. Khalil went on to be a teacher. That's how come you see so many books on the wall."

More like *walls*. I stand there looking at the three walls of books in the room. There must be more than a thousand.

"You're welcome to borrow one," Armstrong says, "as long as you fill out the card."

He shows me a small wooden box like a librarian would have. Inside it's got a few index cards filled out. I look at the names on them: Cecily, Nika, Ebony, Lenai, Charmaine.

"My sisters are my only patrons so far. So feel free if something grabs your eye. That's the shelf of kids' books over there."

He points to one shelf, and I glance through the titles. There are classics like *The Adventures of Tom Sawyer, Kidnapped,* and *Treasure Island*. Fantasy books like *A Wrinkle in Time* and *The Hobbit*. A book called *Tales from Shakespeare* and one called *The Iliad*. So many titles, I can't choose.

"Try this one," Armstrong says, handing me *The Outsiders*.

"What's it about?"

"Well, there's these three boys living on their own because their parents died in a crash. They're part of a gang called the Greasers, and they go against the rich kids in town. There's some violence in it, and some poetry, and a nice friendship between two boys. I think you'll like it, Ross. But I got to warn you it's sad."

"Does somebody die?"

"I'll just say it's a book that tells the truth."

He makes me fill out a card with my name and the title.

We go outside into Armstrong's garden. "The lemon tree and avocado tree, those were Mr. Khalil's idea. He always said it's nice if you can eat from your own yard. I might try artichokes in the fall. It's the right climate zone, you know."

"Where'd you learn so much about gardening?"

"My library. And my friend."

"There's something different about you," I say.

"Since when?"

"Since he died. You seem . . . I don't know . . . older."

Armstrong taps his cheek a few times. "He told me not to grieve him when he's gone. When somebody you feel close to passes, he said, a little piece of them stays behind in you."

We walk around to the porch and sit in two chairs. Patches chases a bird, then gets distracted by his ball. He brings it to Armstrong, who throws it for him.

"Your daddy," Armstrong says, "he okay?"

"He's been sleeping in Andy's room. He has nightmares sometimes."

"Like The Flashbacks. My daddy gets them all the time. Try not to leave him alone when they come."

The sun goes down behind a tall tree in front. We just sit there watching it like we own the place. And the funny thing is, one of us does.

Armstrong

At home the kitchen has been invaded by females finally back from school. Cecily is going on about how she hates algebra. Charmaine is telling Daddy to fix her a snack and being told to fix her own, but when he looks at the twigs she's got for arms, it's not long before he's spreading peanut butter on bread. Nika and Ebony work a pair of click-clacks. Lenai is putting an upside-down fudge cake into the oven. That used to be my favorite kind of cake. Now it's tied with the Neverfail.

Lenai notices Ross right away. "You must be Armstrong's friend from Wonderland," she says, all polite like a firstborn ought to be.

Then she looks at me like I'm doing something wrong.

"Aren't you going to introduce us?"

"Ross," I say, "these are my sisters. Sisters, this is Ross."

"Charlie, actually," he says. "Ross is my last name."

Charmaine looks at him.

"Charlie's a nice name for a boy. I'm Charmaine."

Pretty soon Charlie Ross is surrounded by girls.

"I'm Ebony."

"Nika."

"Cecily."

"Lenai."

He shakes hands with all five. Then I hear Nika and Ebony giggling and whispering together like they're up to no good.

"How come you're so cute, Charlie Ross?" Ebony says.

"I didn't know I was," Ross says.

"That's even cuter."

Ebony lays her dreamy eyes on him. "He spending the night?"

"I doubt it," I say. "He sneaked onto the bus. In for a huge whipping when his daddy finds out."

"Your father doesn't know where you are?" Daddy says.

Ross shakes his head. Daddy hands him the wall phone.

Charlie

I dial Ross Rents. Gwynne answers and puts me right through to my dad. He asks "where in God's name" I am. "Your mother is out of her mind with worry."

All of a sudden I feel terrible. I should have at least called Mom.

I tell him I'm fine. I tell him I'm safe. With Armstrong.

"WHAT?! YOU'RE WHERE?!"

"Armstrong's house."

There's a long silence on the other end.

"Dad?"

He asks for the address. I relay it to him from Mr. Le Rois. Dad says he'll pick me up after work. That's all he says before hanging up.

"Everything okay?" Mr. Le Rois asks.

"Oh, yeah," I say. "No problem. He'll come get me after six."

In the living room, Armstrong shows me this wooden box he made. It's got a slit in the top and a corked hole on the side.

On the front, in his small boxy printing, is a rhyme:

Cussing ain't the nicest thing,
And friends for you it sure don't bring.
But if you really gotta say 'em,
Here's the way you hafta pay 'em:
A mild cuss is just a dime.
A barroom cuss costs a quarter.
For awful cusses you really oughter
Put in the box at least a dollar.

"You raised the prices!" I say.

"Like a good entrepreneur. And the way my sisters talk, Cuss Box is getting rich."

We sit on the floor and open a big bin of wooden toys. We make a little city together, with couch cushions, books, and train tracks winding through. Mr. Le Rois, who apparently can build anything with his hands, has made his kids a world of wood. Locomotives, boxcars, miniature benches, tables, and trees that hold our interest longer than Hot Wheels ever could.

But I'm having a hard time living in our fantasy town. Around every corner, in every saloon, I keep thinking I'll run into an angry sheriff—my dad. What's he going to do to punish me this time? I went against his will. He'll say I wasn't thinking *yet again*.

But I *was* thinking this time. Because when we get home tonight, he'll have to tell Mom what happened. He'll have to tell her what he made me promise not to. I don't care what the punishment is. It's worth it if he'll finally tell.

At 5:30 Patches leaps onto the couch. Armstrong's dad steps into the living room smelling like Windex and wearing his artificial leg. One by one the sisters come in too. Nika—her headband is blue and Ebony's is green—announces, "Mama's home," and now Lenai comes in from the kitchen, wiping her hands on a towel, and Ebony looks up from her schoolbooks, and Cecily turns off her calculator, and Charmaine stands up as the front door opens, and in steps Gracie Le Rois.

She wears a white nurse's uniform, wrinkly at the end of a long day. She sets down a shopping bag and hugs her family one at a time.

Mr. Le Rois gets the last hug. The longest, too.

"We've got ourselves a guest for dinner," he says.

She sees me over his shoulder. "Armstrong," she teases, "did you pick up another stray dog?"

"No, Mama. It's Ross. He followed me home from school."

She smiles at me. "Hello, Charlie."

I tell her that my father is on his way to pick me up.

"There's room at our table if he wants to join us," she says.

She goes down the hall and soon I hear running water through the walls. A few minutes later, Lenai and the twins put the dinner on the table. Armstrong's oldest sister made corn-flake chicken using crushed cereal instead of bread crumbs. And she made green beans from Armstrong's garden, mashed potatoes, and a salad.

Mrs. Le Rois comes to dinner wearing a bright green dress with yellow flowers on it. There is one empty spot at the table, just like she said, and I'm hoping that when my dad shows up, he'll come inside and sit there.

We've just sat down when I hear *hah honk honk, hah honk honk honk, hah hah honk honk hah hah.*

"It's my dad," I say. I get up and walk over to the window.

"Invite him in," Teddy Le Rois says.

At the window, I pull back the curtain and see my father sitting in the Buick. I wave to get his attention. He looks through the windshield at me. I motion for him to come inside.

He grabs a larger piece of air and throws it at the seat next to him.

"Is he coming in?" Armstrong's mom asks.

I stand there seeing my dad through two panes of glass. They're like a telescope turned the wrong way around. He seems farther away than he really is.

Over by the table, everyone is still.

In the car, my father hooks more air, a double grab this time. His finger points to the passenger seat.

I stand at the window. I'm made of stone.

Armstrong

This is what Mr. Khalil would call an "impasse." That's two opinions that don't agree, and neither one's about to budge.

Charlie

He honks again, two angry blasts. I can feel that sound inside my chest. I can feel it in my feet. But they don't move.

Armstrong

I hope he's not planning to die inside that car. Then Charlie Ross will grow up to be a man inside my house—and we don't have a rollaway for him to sleep on. Nika reaches for a piece of chicken. Daddy swats her hand away.

Charlie

Please, Dad.

Armstrong

The trouble with *these* white people is they're stubborn. A daddy tree stump and his son.

"Armstrong, where are you going?"

"Outside to talk to Papa Ross. Before we die of hunger, or he dies of old age."

I don't know what happens past page forty-five of that book Otis was reading, but if I *could* receive a visit from ghosts right now, there's two I'd like by my side. One is Mr. Khalil, who would help me find the right words to say.

The other is Andy Ross, who would help Papa Ross to hear.

I tap on the passenger-side window of the Buick. It rolls partway down.

"Hello, Armstrong," Papa Ross says. "Would you tell Charlie to come on out, please? We have to get home. There's a lot of traffic on the freeway."

"It usually quiets down after seven, Mr. Ross. Besides, we have plenty of food and my parents would really like it if you would join us for dinner."

"Charlie's mom will already have dinner going. Thank your mother for the invitation. Just tell Charlie to come on out."

Now I reach my hand inside the window and lift up the lock. I open the door, get in, and pull the door shut.

I hear a click. I glance down and see that the door just locked from the driver's side. The window goes up again.

"The thing is, Mr. Ross, his feet are pretty much stuck to the floor."

I don't know if it's right or wrong what I'm about to say. But the words just come.

"Charlie told me what happened to you. He needed to tell."

Papa Ross's hands hold tight to the steering wheel. Eyes hold tight to the street.

"And I am so sorry for it."

His head doesn't turn.

"You know," I say, "the night before my first bus ride to your neighborhood, my mama told me we're different and the same. I didn't believe that. But now I know she's right. You and Mrs. Ross lost a son. Charlie lost a brother. I lost my old friend. That's different and the same. Plus, we both got fear. I'm scared someone will pull a gun on me too. Probably it'll be a boy in a gang or a man with a badge. But the fear we carry, that's the same."

His hands drop from the steering wheel to his lap.

"Papa Ross, won't you please come inside our home and eat with my family? It would mean a lot to Charlie. A lot to me, too."

There's a long stretch of quiet, and then a click as the door locks jump back up.

Charlie

After what feels like forever, Armstrong walks in. He walks in with my dad.

"Have you ever tried upside-down fudge cake, Papa Ross?"

"No, Armstrong, I never have."

"Well, get your quarter ready. It's that good."

Dad wipes his feet on the welcome mat. He looks at me.

"We're staying for dinner, Charlie, if that's okay with you."

"Yes, Dad. I'd like that."

He steps into the house and says hello to Armstrong's parents and his sisters. Then he asks to use the phone. He dials Mom to tell her where we are. I hear him say, "Armstrong's house" twice, adding, "I'll explain later. I'll tell you everything later."

He says it to my mom, but he's looking straight at me.

We join the family at the table. Me between Nika and Ebony, my dad between Teddy and Gracie Le Rois.

The food gets passed around, and everyone helps themselves. But I don't have to. Nika scoops mashed potatoes onto my plate from one side, and Ebony adds green beans from the other. I try to tell them I've got enough, but they just keep piling it on.

Across the table, Armstrong is waiting for the mashed potatoes and green beans to be passed to *him*. His eyes bounce between his sisters and me. I just shrug.

Then I hear Teddy Le Rois say to my dad, "That was Morse code your horn blew, wasn't it?"

"You recognized it?"

"A call for soldiers back to base. *Dah dit dit, dah dah dit dit, dah dah dit dit dah dah*. I was a field commander in Korea. With the Seventy-seventh Engineering Corps."

"I was a radioman, third class, in Japan."

Armstrong

Different. And the same.

· 19 ·

TEN PICTURES

Charlie

MY PARENTS STAY UP LATE TALKING. I listen to the sound of their voices through the wall. Mom's goes up and down, fast and slow, soft and loud. Dad's stays steady through all the sharp turns.

At one point she yells, "I'M HIS MOTHER! YOU SHOULD HAVE TOLD ME!"

Then I hear his voice, then hers. His, then hers.

No more yelling. Just vibrations through the wall.

After that it's quiet.

After that I fall asleep.

In the morning, I wake up to Mom sitting on the edge of my bed.

"Charlie," she says. "I'm so sorry I didn't know."

I yawn and rub the sleep from my eyes. "He said you had enough to deal with," I tell her. "He said we shouldn't add one more thing."

"That was wrong. I should have known. You needed me to know."

She makes me promise I won't disappear again like that. "Not on a bike. Not on a bus. Not ever again."

"I promise I won't disappear," I say.

And she says, "I promise I won't either."

She puts her arms around me, and that's when I start to cry. For the first time since Andy died, the tears pour out. A whole year's worth, in wave after wave. I can hardly breathe. I just keep on crying and crying like . . .

Yeah, like a mama's boy.

And the mama whose boy I am holds me. She holds me with all eight of her arms.

In Andy's darkroom Mom sets up the tools she'll need. A bottle opener to pop the canister, a reel to take up the film, and a drum to put it in. She fills a bucket with hot water from the teakettle and cool water from a jug. When the temperature is just right, she tugs on the light bulb chain and suddenly it's pitch-black in here. She snaps open the canister, snips the end off the film, and winds it onto the spool. Once she has the film on the reel and the reel safely inside the drum, she tugs the chain again and the light comes back. She pours in the developer and asks me to rock the drum while she gets the next chemicals ready. The room smells like fresh copies from the ditto machine at school. And like Andy's clothes when he'd work in here.

When enough time has passed, Mom unspools the negatives, rinses them, and hangs them up to dry. While she's filling the trays with new chemicals, we hear footsteps and then a knock on the darkroom door.

"Safe to come in?" Dad asks from the other side.

"Safe to come in," Mom says. I pull open the door. Dad comes in and stands beside me.

"We're ready to print," she says.

Dad shuts the door and snaps on the Mystery Light. That's what Andy called the red light he'd develop by.

Mom slides the strip of negatives into the enlarger, dials up the focus, and does a test strip to get the exposure right. Then she begins to print ten of my brother's favorite things.

The first picture is of Dad on his Vespa. He's wearing his white tennis jacket, an extra can of balls strapped to the rack.

Mom sets a sheet of Kodak paper on the easel, turns the timer to eight seconds, and flicks on the enlarger light.

Andy and I used to love getting rides on the Vespa. All that speed and wind felt like skiing, only uphill. And there was something else. As far as dads go, Marty Ross has never been much of a hugger. But when you're on the Vespa, you have to wrap your arms all the way around him. You have to hug him to hold on.

The enlarger light snaps off. In the red glow of the Mystery Light, I see Dad wipe his eyes.

Mom slides the paper off the easel and drops it into the developer tray. She rocks the tray back and forth for about a minute. The same image we saw on the enlarger plate now comes swimming up in the tray. She moves the print to the stop bath, then to the fixer. Then she rinses the photograph and hangs it up to dry.

Next is a shot of me in our Thinking Tree. Not the nicest angle. He got my butt hanging over a branch.

Number three is a cover from *MAD* magazine. It shows a hand with a finger sticking up—I'll bet you can guess which one—and the headline "The Number One Ecch Magazine." "Ecch" was *MAD*'s word for disgusting. Andy loved his subscription to *MAD*. If you can laugh, he used to say, you can live through anything.

Then there's Kathy. He took her portrait at their make-out fort as the sun was going down. She's got her skateboard in her lap and a daisy in her hair.

Next comes the ski hat Andy wore when he was the Masked Marvel. The print is a double exposure over the Mammoth Mountain trail map.

Six is Mom's Mr. Coffee machine. When he turned ten, Andy started to wake up earlier than the rest of us. Somehow he knew, without ever being asked, to flick the switch for her.

After that comes Dad's KitchenAid stand mixer, the paddle dripping with chocolate frosting. A Neverfail Sunday.

Eight is a portrait Andy took of Mom and Dad and me. We're at the Farmers Market, standing under the bull's horns at Bryan's Pit Barbecue. Instead of *one, two, three . . . SMILE,* it was *one, two, three* . . . *BITE*. Andy caught us with our mouths full of his favorite sandwich, chins covered in dark sauce.

Nine is our back slope in spring, looking down from the neighbors' yard. The calla lilies look like soldiers waving white flags.

The last picture is a giant capital *A* with a Rudolph light on top. It's the radio tower on the hill above the Mulholland Tennis Club, the tallest point in Laurel Canyon. You can see the tower from our Thinking Tree and from way out in the valley. You can see it from the window of an airplane landing at Burbank Airport. Mom calls it our very own Eiffel Tower. Andy hoped to climb it someday all the way to the top.

Maybe now he has.

We watch the tower floating in the fixer tray. Then I realize something and say it out loud.

"I'm not his little brother anymore."

Mom and Dad both look at me.

"From now and forever, I'm older than Andy ever was."

I feel two arms come around me, one from either side.

"Charlie," Mom says, "in many ways, you've been older than Andy for a long time."

We stay awhile in the darkroom. My brother's ten pictures dry on the line.

· 2 0 ·

UP IN LAUREL CANYON

Armstrong

ON THE FIRST DAY of sixth grade, they put us in two lines. Half got Mr. Mitchell, and the lucky half had Mrs. Valentine. Today and all this week, the two lines are back together again. Only one teacher is in charge of graduation, and I'm glad to say that's Mrs. Valentine.

Monday she brings us to the auditorium and sits at an old piano. She tells us it was a gift from the first class to graduate from Wonderland back in 1932. She says there's a secret scratched on its back, and asks who wants to come see what the secret is.

Forty-two hands rocket up.

"Armstrong," she calls.

Even if you aren't in Mrs. Valentine's class, she knows your name.

I step through all the pretzel legs to the front, then slide into the space between the piano and the wall. On the back of the piano, somebody has whittled the words to a song.

"It's a song," I say.

"Can you make out the lyrics?"

They've been there forty-three years, but I can see them plain as day.

"'Up in Laurel Canyon,'" I read aloud, "'there is a little school./ It is known as Wonderland,/ Where all sixth-graders rule.'"

"Those are the opening words to our school song," Mrs. Valentine says. "Forty-three graduating classes have sung it on a bright or foggy or rainy day in June. On Thursday you will be the forty-fourth."

She opens the piano and starts to play. "First me, then you.

Up in Laurel Canyon, there is a little school.
It is known as Wonderland, where all sixth-graders rule.
Wonderland, Wonderland, friends so dear and true.
Wonderland, Wonderland, we'll remember you."

She leads us through the next verse and one more after that. On the second time through, most of us have it down. By the third, we're sounding pretty good.

Charlie

On Tuesday Mrs. Valentine hands us blank squares of card-board. She tells us to write down our predictions for the future. "Not for yourselves, but for a friend. Where will they live when they grow up? What job will they have? Will they be married? With children of their own?"

The kind of questions that make your head hurt. I pick Armstrong and he picks me. We write down our predictions and make them small enough to fit on one square, so that when the squares get put together, copied into programs, and given to our families on Graduation Day, they'll see we're a class of future veterinarians, rock stars, painters, lawyers, doctors, astronauts, or, in Otis's case, a psychologist, and in Shelley's, an architect and a violinist and a teacher and a mom.

The squares were all kept secret until today, Graduation Day, when we're placing the programs on the folding chairs.

Armstrong stops to look at one. He doesn't like what he sees.

"*Entrepreneur?!* Ross, I plan on being president of the United States."

"But you already started your first business," I say. "There aren't a lot of kids our age who've done that."

"You don't think I can be president?"

"I never said that. But you can only be president for eight years. What'll you do the rest of the time?"

He thinks about that, then shrugs. "Entrepreneur, huh? Well, at least you spelled it right."

I flip a few pages to see what he put down for my future. "A *writer*?"

"Didn't you tell me that when your brother was sick and couldn't read, he'd ask you for a story? And after the story, he'd feel better? Well, if you can help a boy forget he has asthma, think what you can do for the rest of the world."

"But I'm planning to be a guard in the NBA."

Armstrong's upper lip starts to quiver. "I hate to burst your basketball, Ross, but I don't think we'll be seeing your face on an NBA trading card. You've got Zayde Moishe in your genes. I doubt they need a rabbi on the Lakers."

Well, I stand by my predictions. For Armstrong and for me.

Armstrong

After we set the programs on the chairs, we line up outside just like we practiced, and soon the people start to come. There's Mr. Orr, Ross's bus driver, side by side with Miss Charles, a kindergarten teacher, who must be his sweetheart because he just offered her an Andes mint. And there's Mrs.

Gaines over by Mrs. Wilson, both of them wearing pearls today. And here come Mr. Mitchell and Mrs. Valentine. Everybody two by two like they're stepping off the Ark. Me and Ross are jostling each other for a place in line, Shelley behind us, holding Ross's hand. And I see Papa Ross and Mrs. Ross, holding hands too.

Now a long yellow bus swings in through the open school gate. Mrs. Wilson arranged for the transportation so our families wouldn't have to come by taxi or by car. The bus hisses to a stop, the engine shudders down, the door flaps open.

First ones off are my five sisters. Then come Daddy and Mama, real slow. After them it's Otis's mom and his grandma and all nine of his cousins. Alma's three brothers and the rest of her clan. Dezzy's family — they could've filled a bus of their own. And the families of some of the younger kids who traveled with us this year to Wonderland. Mrs. Wilson wanted to invite all the families who came on Opportunity Busing because this was the first year.

People start to find seats. I notice Daddy talking to Papa Ross, who holds a brown bag. Then the two of them make their way over to the boys' bathroom. I wonder what they've got going on.

Oh, and here comes Mrs. Gaines to say hello.

"Armstrong. Charlie."

"Hi, Mrs. Gaines," we say.

Lenai and Charmaine and Cecily and Ebony and Nika

and Mama all walk up. Patches is here too, in Charmaine's arms. Since Mr. Khalil passed, we can't leave him alone or he howls like he's calling the old man.

Whose absence here today is the one thing I'm feeling sad on.

"Mrs. Gaines," I say, "I would like you to meet my family. These are my five sisters and my mom."

"Armstrong has certainly livened things up this year," Mrs. Gaines says. "I have expended no small amount of ink on his behalf." And then she adds, "We've been blessed to have him."

"Thank you, ma'am," Mama says. "We feel the same way."

"Say hello to my dog, too, Mrs. Gaines. He's real friendly."

She leans down and pats his head. Then Patches lets loose like he knows what she had for breakfast. He's licking her hand. Licking her chin. Licking up her cheeks, too. Mrs. Gaines is laughing so hard you can see her fillings are made of gold.

"Wha—what's his name?" she says when she finally gets a breath.

"Oh," I say. "Well, that's Patches."

"Patches? Patches . . . Why, is this the same dog that —Oh, LORD!"

Imagine a black woman turning white as a ghost! She throws back her head and dashes off to the girls' bathroom.

INCIDENT REPORT

Submitted by: Edwina Gaines, Yard Supervisor at
Wonderland Avenue School

Date of Incident: Thursday, June 12, 1975

Time: 2:47 p.m.

Location: the girls' bathroom

We experienced a delay of graduation this
afternoon, and I must confess I was the cause.
Among the friends and family milling about the
upper yard in anticipation of the ceremony, there
was one dog. Now, a dog at graduation might be
reason enough for an Incident Report, but this one
in particular caused quite the hullaballoo. His name
is Patches, and you will recall from a previous
report (October 10, 1974) that this was the same dog
responsible for my taking a rare day off.

I myself made the connection while he was
enthusiastically licking my cheek. Overcome with
disgust and horror, I ran into the girls' bathroom to
recompose myself. While trembling behind the bar-
rier of a closed stall, I heard a voice call out.

"Mrs. Gaines," it said, "this is Armstrong Le
Rois, stepping into the girls' bathroom."

"Oh, Armstrong, please!" I cried. "Leave the dog
outside!"

"Now, don't be afraid of Patches," he said. "He's safe in my sister's arms. Besides, it's time I told you the truth about him. What you put down in that Incident Report was lies. All lies. At the time, Mr. Khalil was healthy and breathing the same air as you and me. Patches never had a lick of a dead man's face."

"But why did you tell such a dreadful tale?"

And out poured the truth that the boy had been holding in all year. He was hiding in the bathroom from a test, he said, when I walked in and found him. He had to invent something, and the story about the old man and the dog is what came to mind.

Then he told me it was wrong. And he was sorry for it. "Extra sorry," he said, "because a month ago, Mr. Khalil really did die."

He began to sob. Not the crocodile tears he cried back in October, but real ones, born of true grief. I unlatched the door to my stall and stepped out. Armstrong stood weeping over by the sink.

"Were you very close?" I asked.

He sucked back tears. "He was like a grandfather to me, Mrs. Gaines. Loved me like a grandson, too. Did you know I'm a landlord now? Mr. Khalil left me his house. My daddy and I are fixing it up to rent so I can save for college."

And telling out loud how that old man had given

him a future . . . well, that brought forth the tears again.

"That's the sweetness of life, Armstrong," I said, patting his shoulder. "And the bitter. That you can love somebody one day, and another they're gone."

I cranked out a good ten inches of paper towel and tore it off for him. "How lucky you are to have known him, and loved him."

I handed him the paper towel. "Now, then," I said, "how are you going to fulfill that man's dream for you to go to college, if you don't step out of here and graduate from elementary?"

Whereupon Armstrong dried his eyes, and together we stepped out of the girls' bathroom, both of us feeling restored.

This concludes the final Incident Report of the year by Edwina Gaines, Yard Supervisor of Wonderland Avenue School.

Next year I'll be moving on to Crossing Guard.

Charlie

While Armstrong is in the girls' bathroom trying to rescue Mrs. Gaines, I realize I'm holding Shelley's hand and all it would take is one tug to lead her away from the line and around to the back of the building, where we might have a minute, maybe two, of privacy.

So I tug.

And we run.

"Where are we going, Charlie?" she says. "We'll miss graduation."

"No we won't."

Behind the building I lift a strand of Shelley's hair and tuck it behind the ear where that forty-seventh freckle is. She's wearing new glasses today, boxy black frames perfectly straight on her nose.

"I really like your new glasses," I tell her.

"Is that why you dragged me over here?"

"No," I say.

Then I kiss her.

Only this time it's not just on the lips.

She does that twirly thing to the back of my hair, and I hold my hand behind her neck, and—well, what happens next is private. All I can say is, she tastes like candy and lip-gloss and the end of sixth grade. And I think, it wouldn't be so bad to go on kissing past graduation, past summer, all the way to junior high.

"Ross."

Armstrong's head pops around the corner. "Hurry up," he says. "Line's starting to move."

Shelley and I make our way along the wall. We keep on kissing until we turn the corner.

Armstrong

After the speeches and the walks across stage and the diplomas and the cheers, we stand together and sing the Wonderland song for the forty-fourth time. Then we all pour out onto the upper yard for pastries and coffee and music from the school's small band. Otis plays trumpet, Alex is on drums, and Alma and Dezzy are singing a duet of "Sunshine of My Life."

And then a crazy thing happens. Parents, grandparents, brothers, and sisters—old, young, and in between—all start to dance.

Nobody closer than Ross and Shelley.

Nobody slower than Papa Ross and the Mrs.

Nobody more tangled up than my five sisters and me.

And nobody, I'm surprised to say, more beautiful than my own mama and daddy.

It's like he's dancing on a borrowed leg.

"Daddy," I say, "what happened to you? How in this world can you dance like that?"

"I can dance like this," he says, "on account of my new stump sock. It's got gel and Velcro, and it gives me support without the pain. And it was custom-made for me by the father of your friend. The man you call Papa Ross."

He lifts Mama's hand and twirls her under his arms. I

look over little kids' heads, past Mrs. Valentine's shoulder, and I find Papa Ross's eyes. He smiles at me, then pivots away to dance with his wife.

If there's one thing you can't do on this planet, Mr. Khalil once told me, it's defy physics. What goes up must come down. Matter cannot be destroyed or created. Every action has an equal and opposite reaction. And though you might want to, you can't stop time.

"Sunshine of My Life" comes to an end.

Otis's grandma tips the coffeepot, but no more coffee comes out.

The folding chairs go *clap, clap, clap* as they get folded up.

Car doors answer with a *clunk, clunk, clunk* as people get in.

Pretty soon the yard is emptied out, the guests on their way home, the graduation on its way to being a memory.

"Armstrong, time to get on the bus."

That's Otis, with his head poking out a side window. Five more heads poke out. They look just like me, only older and girls.

"Armstrong," Lenai says, "the bus has to leave."

The engine rumbles to life. I take a last look at this schoolyard I stepped onto almost a year ago, and I think to myself, I'm glad I had the opportunity to come.

Then I turn toward the bus, but a voice calls out to me.

"Armstrong, wait!"

Charlie Ross comes running up with something in his hand.

Charlie

"There was one more shot on Andy's roll," I tell him. "My mom took it the night you slept over. She printed it this morning, for you."

I hand him a photograph of the two of us. I'm on the rollaway with my mouth wide open — probably snoring — and the covers all twisted around my legs. Armstrong's in my bed, peaceful and asleep. He smiles now at the picture.

"Mine to keep?"

"Yours to keep."

He looks at me and says, "Think we'll see each other again?"

It's the question I've been afraid to ask. Mrs. Wilson once told us this was an experimental year for Opportunity Busing. If it goes well, they'll expand the program to more schools. Next year the buses might even run both ways. But right now nobody knows for sure.

"We can get together over the summer," I say. "We can get together during breaks."

"That'd be nice, Ross. That'd be real nice." And then he adds, "But just in case . . ."

With a swift jerk of his hands, Armstrong rips the picture in half. I gasp like he just ripped *me* in half.

"You hold on to me. I'll hold on to you. Someday we'll tape us back together again."

He tucks the picture of me into his pocket. I tuck the one of him into mine.

Our hands come out and clasp together like we're going to arm-wrestle — but we're not about to start *that* again. Instead, they slide into a handshake and pull back until our fingers meet, like a hinge.

Armstrong tugs me toward him. We put our arms around each other and stand there like two trunks grown into a single tree. The only tree in the Canyon, it feels like. The only one in the world.

And then,

because the sun has gone down,

because all the chairs have been folded up and taken away,

because the parking lot is empty,

because the bus has to leave,

because the janitor has to lock the gate,

because we're the last ones on the yard,

because we can't stop time,

because we have to,

we let go.

GRATITUDE

Armstrong & Charlie would not exist without the inspiration, guidance, and guardianship of the following people:

The students who rode into my life in the 1970s on a long yellow bus—you broke down barriers, opened hearts and minds, and widened our Laurel Canyon world.

My real-life brothers, Michael and Danny Frank, who were okay with being killed off in fiction.

My father, Marty Frank, who allowed me to write about his pain.

My mother, Merona Frank, who read an early draft on her cell phone and gave the perfect blend of encouragement and advice, especially about Charlie's mom.

Michael Frank, brother in both blood and craft, who dug deep into the psychology of these characters as no one else can, and who was essential in getting the book out the door.

Maira Kalman for a much-appreciated introduction to Charlotte Sheedy.

Charlotte, who gave the manuscript to Kevin O'Connor.

Kevin, whose candor, clarity, and diamond-cutting skills made *Armstrong & Charlie* the book that it is.

Margaret Raymo at Houghton Mifflin Harcourt Books for *all* Readers; you were my dream editor, and you came true.

Thanks also to the whole team at HMH — Betsy Groban, Mary Wilcox, Linda Magram, Karen Walsh, and Lisa DiSarro for helping launch the book and making the writer feel so welcome; to the logical, hawk-eyed Susan Buckheit for copyediting the book; and to Sharismar Rodriguez and Andy Smith for designing and drawing a cover that jumps off the shelf into a reader's arms.

To my students at Le Lycée Français de Los Angeles, who, over many years, have kept me "au courant" with the devilish and delightful workings of the middle school brain; to my aunt, Harriet Frank, Jr., an early and ardent champion of this book; my mother-in-law, Nana Bette, who has been asking for a long time for something of mine to read; my children, Sophie, Sam, and Mia, for tolerating a dad who stands at the kitchen counter typing all the time; and to my wife, Julie, who lives patiently with the voices in my head.

Finally to you, Reader, for your gift of attention and time.